“What’s going

“Well,” Gabriel said, topping the steps, “it appears Aggie has decided you’re her new handler.”

Confusion creased Jillian’s brow. “I don’t understand.”

“You know how I said she belonged to one of my clients?”

She nodded.

“Aggie wasn’t just his pet. She was his service dog. He suffered from PTSD. Aggie could sense when he was having or about to have a panic attack. And it appears she wants to help you.”

“What does that mean?”

He shrugged. “She wants to be your dog. To live with you. Go to work with you.”

“I—I don’t know what to say.”

“I think she could be a great asset to you. So what do you say?”

Jillian knelt beside the dog. “Like you, I don’t believe in coincidence.” She cupped Aggie’s chin. “I think God brought the two of us together for a reason. So, Aggie, if you’re set on helping me, who am I to say no?”

Standing again, Jillian peered up at him, looking almost bashful. “Thank you, Gabriel. For everything.”

Award-winning author **Mindy Obenhaus** lives on a ranch in Texas with her husband, two sassy pups, and countless cattle and deer. She's passionate about touching readers with biblical truths in an entertaining, and sometimes adventurous, manner. When she's not writing, you'll usually find her in the kitchen, spending time with family or roaming the ranch. She'd love to connect with you via her website, mindyobenhaus.com.

Books by Mindy Obenhaus

Love Inspired

Hope Crossing

The Cowgirl's Redemption
A Christmas Bargain
Loving the Rancher's Children
Her Christmas Healing

Bliss, Texas

A Father's Promise
A Brother's Promise
A Future to Fight For
Their Yuletide Healing

Visit the Author Profile page at LoveInspired.com for more titles.

ISBN-13: 978-1-335-59848-6

Her Christmas Healing

For questions and comments about the quality of this book, please contact us at CustomerService@Harlequin.com.

Love Inspired
22 Adelaide St. West, 41st Floor
Toronto, Ontario M5H 4E3, Canada
www.LoveInspired.com

Printed in U.S.A.

Her Christmas Healing

Mindy Obenhaus

To appoint unto them that mourn in Zion, to give unto them beauty for ashes, the oil of joy for mourning, the garment of praise for the spirit of heaviness; that they might be called trees of righteousness, the planting of the Lord, that he might be glorified.

—*Isaiah* 61:3

For Your Glory, Lord

Acknowledgments

To Dr. Michael and Kathie Ridlen, thank you for so willingly sharing your knowledge with me. And to Susan Chandler, you have opened my eyes to the world of a library director. Thank you.

Chapter One

A baby changes everything.

Jillian McKenna had heard the adage before, but as she stood in the parking lot of the Hope Crossing Senior Living Community Thursday afternoon, the trunk and back seat of her Honda Accord stuffed to the gills, she couldn't agree more.

After assessing her surroundings, she stretched, savoring the mid-October air. This had always been her favorite time of year. When summer's heat finally yielded to more moderate temperatures that beckoned one to enjoy the outdoors. And, perhaps, now that she was going to be living in Hope Crossing, the tiny Texas town that had always been a haven for her, she might find the courage to do that once again.

Her hand settled atop her slightly swollen belly. Five months had passed since that morning she'd opted to jog without her running partner. The days that followed had been some of the most difficult of her life. But God had granted her beauty for ashes. A gift that, at thirty-eight years of age, Jillian thought she'd never receive. So even though her carefully crafted life had been upended and her confidence shaken, and her family routinely questioned her decisions, she'd embarked on this new journey God had set before her. One that had her trading her dream job at the Dallas library for that of library director in this map-dot town. Because Hope Crossing had something Dallas didn't—Ida Mae Crowley.

Eager to see her grandmother, Jillian sent her mother a brief text to let her know she'd arrived safely, then locked her car before continuing onto the sidewalk that led to the rocking-chair-lined porch spanning the front of the red-brick building. Though the facility was small, it boasted fifteen assisted-living apartments, along with a skilled nursing wing for those who needed a higher level of care. Something rather unique for a town with a population of less than four hundred, but a godsend for many in the area who wanted to keep their loved ones nearby.

She reached for the door and continued into the lobby with its gleaming brass chandelier and floors reminiscent of reclaimed wood. A pair of black-and-white-checked wingback chairs separated by a distressed side table created a cozy nook along the wall opposite the reception desk, while an abundance of autumnal decor gave the place a nice homey feel.

"Hi, Jillian." Carrie, the receptionist, appeared from the office behind the counter as Jillian approached. "Ms. Ida Mae told me you'd be in today." The woman in her midforties with short brown hair perched a hand on her hip. "I still can't believe you'd trade life in the city for little ol' Hope Crossing. I mean, in Dallas you have everything you could ever want right around the corner. Shopping, dining, movie theaters. Now you'll have to drive a minimum of twenty minutes for any of those things."

Picking up the pen next to the sign-in sheet, Jillian said, "What about Plowman's?" The quirky little store sold everything from tractor parts to homemade baked goods and almost anything in between.

"Oh, please." Carrie waved off the comment as Jillian added her name and check-in time to the list.

Returning the pen to the counter, Jillian said, "City life has its conveniences. But there's a lot to be said about living in a place where everyone knows everyone, and they all look out for each other."

Turning, Jillian continued on to the assisted-living wing. Since it was nearing one o'clock, lunch should be over, meaning Grandmama would, likely, be back in her room. Yet as Jillian was about to head down Grandmama's hallway, she heard someone say, "There's my girl!"

Jillian twisted toward her grandmother's voice to discover the octogenarian waving from one of the square tables in the dining room and started that way. Though Grandmama's once-auburn hair had turned a vibrant white, she still kept it styled in a sleek ballerina bun. And despite topping out at a mere four foot eleven, her maternal grandmother had always been a giant in Jillian's book.

"Hello, Grandmama." She stooped to embrace the woman who'd been her rock in recent months.

"Oh, my Jilly. It's so good to have you here. I've been counting the days."

Jillian's eyes closed as she savored the affection. Grandmama was the only person who had never questioned Jillian's decision to keep her baby. Instead, she'd said, "God calls each of us to a different path. So long as you're doing what He's called you to do, it doesn't matter what anyone else thinks." Then she'd added, "You stick to your guns, Jilly. God and I will be with you every step of the way."

Finally her grandmother released her hold to peer up at Jillian through wire-rimmed bifocals.

"Those dark circles tell me you haven't been resting well."

Jillian straightened. "I've been busy packing." Grandmama didn't need to know about the insomnia that kept her awake most nights.

To her grandmother's left, Milly Vaughn nodded in Jillian's direction, her brown eyes sparkling. "Well, hello, doll."

"Hello, Ms. Milly." She smiled at the silver-haired woman she'd known all her life. Not only were the two older women best friends since childhood, they'd been next-door neighbors for as long as Jillian could remember. "How are you?"

"I'm doing very well, dear." The older woman gave her a visual once-over, pausing briefly on Jillian's waistline before darting to her face.

Panic washed over Jillian, rendering her speechless. Despite reaching a point where she could no longer hide her pregnancy, she wasn't necessarily ready to discuss it either.

Though, she supposed she'd better get ready, if for no other reason than she was forcing Grandmama to keep her secret, too. And that wasn't fair to her.

"You remember Gabriel." Milly motioned to her left.

Jillian suddenly found it difficult to breathe.

Gabriel Vaughn. Milly's grandson. How had she not noticed him?

Over the last couple of years, Jillian had come to realize that the outgoing, immature boy who was a year younger than her had grown into a compassionate—not to mention handsome—veterinarian who now resided in Milly's house, a lovely single-story Victorian identical to and right next door to Grandmama's. When Jillian would come to town to visit Grandmama, she and Gabriel would often take the grandmas out for lunch or dinner. And as their friendship grew, they began spending even more time together, just her and Gabriel. Even dancing the night away at the Hope Crossing Fair and Rodeo last year. He was fun to be with, and their connection was unmistakable. And perhaps for the first time ever, Jillian had found herself losing her heart.

Until that morning in May when her life was changed forever. Since then, shame had her avoiding his phone calls as well as the man himself when she'd come to interview for the library director position last month.

Willing her voice to remain steady, she forced a smile. "Yes. Of course. Hello, Gabriel."

"Jillian." He nodded, his short brown hair slightly mussed, as though he'd recently dragged his fingers through it the way he so often did. But his green eyes seemed to bore a hole right through her as if searching for answers to the countless questions he, no doubt, had.

Then she thoughtlessly placed a self-conscious hand to her belly. And his gaze followed.

Heat crept up her neck. Her secret was out. And she could only imagine what he and Ms. Milly must think.

"Pull up a chair, Jilly." Grandmama motioned to the empty one between her and Gabriel. "Since we're all together, we may as well take a minute to discuss the Christmas Bazaar."

Jillian eased into the cushioned seat, rubbing her hands along her denim-covered thighs. Funny, she'd never been nervous around Gabriel before. Though, it wasn't the fact that he was a man that had her on edge. It was because he was a man who deserved an explanation. And because of the shame that had held her captive since her assault, she wasn't sure when she'd be ready to give him one.

Suddenly, something wet touched her hand, startling her. She gasped and shrank back to discover two dark eyes staring at her from beneath the table.

The chocolate-brown poodle inched toward her and set its head in her lap.

Sucking in a breath, she placed a shaky hand atop the soft curls between the canine's ears, fighting for her composure. "H-hello there. What's your name?"

"Agatha."

Though her attention remained on the dog, Jillian could feel Gabriel watching her. She dared a glance his way. "Not your typical dog's name."

"No." Crossing his arms, a move that only accentuated the large biceps beneath his maroon polo shirt, he continued to stare at her. "That's why we call her Aggie."

Aware he'd gone to college and veterinary school at Texas A&M, she said, "A nod to your alma mater?"

"Yes. However, I didn't name her. She belonged to a client who passed away a month ago. His family wasn't interested in keeping the dog."

"Aww." Jillian rubbed Aggie more vigorously, and not only because she was fond of dogs. It also distracted her from Gabriel. "How could they turn away a sweet thing like you?"

Grandmama cleared her throat. "Regarding the bazaar."

"Sorry." Like a student caught goofing off in class, Jillian straightened, giving the woman her full attention. Though, when Aggie encouraged Jillian to continue petting her, she readily gave in, determined to keep her mind off Gabriel.

"Before I go any further, I want to remind you both that this is setting up to be one of the biggest fundraisers we've ever done. We want this event to be a success for the youth group, so they'll have plenty of funds for their mission trip next summer."

"Remind me again how this bazaar is supposed to play out." Gabriel looked from one grandmother to the other.

"Of course, dear." Milly tucked her chin-length bob behind one ear. "Folks donate new or gently used items that will then be sold at the bazaar at deeply discounted prices. The community saves money on their Christmas shopping, and Lord willing, the youth will be well on their way to their funding goal."

"Indeed." Grandmama nodded. "And while the students will be doing their share of the work, we want the two of you to oversee things." She waggled a finger from Jillian to Gabriel and back again.

"Shouldn't that be the youth minister's job?" Gabriel lifted a brow.

"Ricky will be involved to a point," Grandmama continued, "but he's a busy man, what with three youngsters and his wife going through cancer treatments. He doesn't need anything else on his plate. Besides, the bazaar was *our* idea." Her pride was obvious in her smile. "And it's going to require more oversight than selling hot cocoa at the Christmas-tree farm like they did last year. We're going to need as many volunteers as possible. People to assist with setup, cashiers, people willing to help shoppers choose the right gift, gift wrapping, and the list goes on.

"Milly and I have been acting as hunters, contacting businesses and individuals, getting them to commit to donating goods or services, and the response has been outstanding. Pastor will be putting out a call for more volunteers in church Sunday, and we'll have a meeting next Wednesday night. But what we need right now are a couple of gatherers."

"Gatherers?" Worry laced Gabriel's tone.

"Someone to collect the donated goods," Milly interjected.

"What sort of stuff are we talking about?" Gabriel sounded more than a little skeptical.

"Handmade candles, gift certificates—" Grandmama ticked the items off on her arthritic fingers "—handcrafted furniture, jewelry, clothing, home decor items, quilts and countless other things I can't remember without my list."

"All that from Hope Crossing?" Jillian was impressed.

Grandmama waved a hand. "And the surrounding areas. Round Top, Brenham."

"The bazaar isn't until December." Gabriel leaned forward, perching his elbows on the table. "Where are we supposed to store the stuff?"

"At the church. They've got a large storage area in the youth barn."

Jillian's insides turned, and it had nothing to do with the baby. Why would Grandmama ask her to go around picking up items? Jillian rubbed Aggie harder as the dog pressed against her leg. Six months ago it might not have bothered her. Now the thought of going to unfamiliar places by herself was a terrifying prospect.

With Aggie licking her hand, Jillian said, "Grandmama, I'm not too keen on traveling the countryside by myself. Besides, I have a small car."

"I don't expect you to go alone, Jilly. We want the two of you to work as a team. To be our representatives."

Jillian was fairly certain Gabriel had no interest in being on a team with her. Not after the way she'd dismissed him without reason. At least from his perspective.

"When do you want us to start doing this?" He eyed his grandmother.

"As soon as possible." She smiled.

"That's kind of unfair to drop that on Jillian when she just got here."

That was so like Gabriel to think of others. Unless he was looking for an excuse to go it alone.

"Next week is fine. That reminds me." Grandmama reached into her pocket, then leaned toward Jillian. "Here's the house key."

"Thank you."

Cocking her head, Milly eyed Jillian across the table. "Gabriel made sure Ida Mae's place is all ready for you."

He cleared his throat. "The air conditioner is on, and so is the hot-water heater."

"He also mowed the lawn," said Milly.

Jillian looked at Gabriel, feeling like the most horrible person in the world. "You didn't have to do that." Nor did she expect it after the way she'd treated him. That was so like Gabriel, though. Always quick to offer a helping hand. Even if they hadn't spoken in months. But then, if her family couldn't comprehend her decision to keep a stranger's baby, how could she expect Gabriel to understand?

"No big deal." He shrugged. "I've been doing it since your grandmother moved out."

"Still, I appreciate it." Eager to escape, Jillian gave Aggie a final pat and stood. "I have a lot of unloading to do, so I should run."

"Understood." Grandmama pushed to her feet and hugged Jillian.

"Good to see both of you." She addressed Milly and Gabriel, before lowering her gaze. "And it was very nice to meet you, Aggie."

With a final wave, Jillian made her way back to the reception area, trying not to think about the curiosity in Gabriel's gaze every time he looked at her.

Once outside, she visually scrutinized the area, spotting Gabriel's veterinary truck. Evidently she wasn't as perceptive as she thought. Otherwise she would have noticed it when she arrived.

"Jillian."

Though she wanted to keep going, her steps slowed at Gabriel's voice. She turned as he approached, Aggie on a leash at his side.

Shoulders squared, his chin held high, nostrils flared, he stared down at her. "You know, you could have at least let me know you were in a relationship."

She slowly drew in a breath. "That would've been easier, I suppose. Except I wasn't in a relationship."

Those green eyes she'd once lost herself in darted between her face and her abdomen.

"And before you ask—" a protective hand covered her baby "—it wasn't a *fling* or a one-night stand either."

His muscles tensed, making his biceps grow even larger. "I think it's safe to say immaculate conception is off the table."

She glowered. She understood that he was upset, but now it was as if he never even knew her. And it was as infuriating as it was painful.

Aggie looked up at Jillian, and she got the feeling that the dog was more than just a pretty face. Could she sense the tension between Jillian and Gabriel?

Unwilling to stand there and be the target of any more of his verbal darts, Jillian turned and continued to her car, praying he'd be at work all afternoon and she'd have everything unloaded before he got home. Because she had no desire to see Gabriel again until it was absolutely necessary.

Thunder clapped just before one the next morning, rattling the windows in Gabriel's bedroom. If he hadn't already been awake, that would've done it for sure. He'd been in a foul mood all day, and now the lingering turmoil prevented him from sleeping.

For years, Doc Grinnell had been claiming he was ready to retire and let Gabriel take over the veterinary clinic. A transition Gabriel was more than ready to make. Doc wasn't getting any younger. At eighty-one, the longtime vet should be enjoying retirement. Sadly, since the passing of his wife last year, he spent even more time at the clinic.

But the way things stood now, Gabriel's greatest fear was that something would happen to Doc, and his kids—who all lived in Houston or Austin and, to Gabriel's knowledge, were unaware of his and Doc's agreement—would sell the practice right out from under him.

So when Doc asked him to come in early this morning so they could talk, Gabriel prayed this would finally be the day. Instead, the man had only wanted to discuss—and shoot down—Gabriel's suggestion they switch from injectables to gas anesthesia for surgeries. Even when Gabriel had noticed the man seemed to be in pain and suggested he go home and rest, Doc, who'd been his mentor for as long as Gabriel could remember, simply shrugged him off.

And then there was Jillian. One of the few women who'd not only captured his attention but actually seemed interested in him as more than just a friend. Or so he'd thought until she'd quit communicating with him only weeks before the town's annual fair and rodeo this past June. An event they'd enjoyed last year and had planned to attend again. Then she backed out—via text message, no less—and he hadn't heard from her since, no matter how many times he'd reached out.

Sure, he'd known she'd be arriving today. But he wasn't prepared to see her at the assisted living, looking as beautiful as ever, her auburn hair tumbling around her shoulders—and pregnant. No wonder she'd dismissed him.

What he couldn't understand was what she was

doing here. She'd always said she could never live in Hope Crossing. That Dallas was her home. Yet here she was, ready to step into the role of director at the town's library, according to the grandmas. Now they expected him to work with Jillian on the bazaar? And what was up with the baby's father?

Maybe if you hadn't called her out and put her on the defensive, she might have been more forthcoming.

And there was the real reason he had yet to get any sleep.

Another crack of thunder had him flopping onto his other side. Until he felt Aggie's hot breath on his face.

"What is it, girl? You can't sleep either?"

She continued to stare at him. Let out a low whine.

"Really? Are you sure you want to go out now? You'll get all wet."

The dog barked.

"Okay, okay." He tossed his covers aside and followed the canine into the kitchen. "Make it quick," he said as he opened the side door for her.

Aggie trotted outside, pausing on the covered porch, nose in the air, before dashing down the wooden steps. That's when Gabriel noticed the kitchen light on in the house across the drive.

Determined not to dwell on Jillian, he went into the bathroom and searched the medicine cabinet for some melatonin. Unable to locate any, he returned to his bedroom to check the drawer in his nightstand.

He rummaged through cold-medicine packets, cough drops, books he had yet to read—"Aha!"

He was about to punch a tablet from the blister pack when his phone rang. Since veterinarians sometimes received after-hours emergency calls, he wasn't surprised. Though, given the weather, he wasn't too keen on going anywhere. Not that he had a choice.

Then he saw Jillian's name on the screen. He hated the way his traitorous heart raced with anticipation. The same way it had when they were still dating-yet-not-really-dating.

Lightning flashed, illuminating the room. And as the thunder followed, he tapped the screen and said, "Hello?"

"There's something or someone outside my kitchen door," Jillian's panic-filled voice whispered in his ear.

Before he could think better of it, he said, "I'll be right there." He rushed back into the kitchen and out the door, his bare feet splashing through puddles while rain soaked his T-shirt.

Lightning streaked across the night sky, propelling him up the steps and onto Jillian's covered porch at the side of the house, where he found Aggie sitting next to the kitchen door.

"What are you doing here?"

The dog whined and pawed at the screen.

Gabriel knocked. "Jillian, it's me."

She opened the door, her hair mussed as she clutched the lapels of the fuzzy pink robe she was wearing. Her blue eyes were wide, her face pale, and her body trembled. She looked terrified.

Unable to stop himself, he said, "May I come in?"

Her nod was almost imperceptible, but she released the old-fashioned hook-and-eye latch and pushed the screen door open as a gust of wind whipped rain against his back.

Aggie promptly forced her way inside to stand beside Jillian. She even pressed against the woman's leg. Something the dog didn't do with most people. Only those who needed her assistance. Because Aggie wasn't an ordinary dog. She was a trained professional. One who hadn't been needed since her handler passed away. But why would Jillian need a psychiatric service dog?

As she closed the door behind him, he said, "That was Aggie you heard scratching. Sorry about that. I had no idea she'd come over here."

Thunder boomed, seemingly right over the house, making the old windows shudder almost as much as Jillian.

Aggie stayed with her as she turned to face him. And as Jillian's hand fell to the dog's dampened head, her pinched expression relaxed a notch.

Still feeling like a jerk for his behavior this afternoon, he met Jillian's skittish gaze. "About earlier." Dragging his fingers through his now-damp hair, he let go a sigh. "I'm sorry. I shouldn't have laid into you like that. You don't owe me any explanations for anything."

"Actually… I do." She hauled in a shaky breath. "You're wet." After reaching into the laundry room to her right, she handed him a towel. "Would you care for some chamomile tea? They say it helps you sleep." Her smile was weak, to say the least.

"Sounds good."

After drying his hair, he draped the towel over his shoulders and pulled out one of four wooden chairs at the matching round table while she added tea bags to two cups, then watched as she poured hot water from a red kettle that sat atop the white stove. And Aggie remained at Jillian's side the entire time.

"I'm sorry if I woke you," she finally said.

"Not a chance with all that thunder." In addition to the guilt that had been prodding him all night.

Her hands shook as she picked up the two mugs, bringing him out of his seat.

As the towel fell to the floor, he said, "Let me get those."

He settled the cups on the table while she eased into the chair next to his.

Aggie sat beside her, resting her chin on Jillian's lap.

Jillian wrapped her long, slender fingers around her mug and stared at the steaming liquid. "First of all, I want you to know that my severing communication between us had nothing to do with you."

Lifting his own cup, he couldn't help the snort that escaped. "Isn't that what they all say?"

She sucked in a breath and moved one hand to rub Aggie's neck. "I'm sorry. There's no easy way to say this."

"Don't worry. I can take it." Even though he had no idea what *it* might be.

"It's not you I'm worried about."

Setting his tea on the table again, he studied the woman next to him. This was not the Jillian he'd come to know. The one who'd always been confident, outgoing and vivacious. Instead, anxiety carved lines between her eyebrows, and her shoulders hunched, as though she was carrying the weight of the world.

"Hey, you don't have to tell me if you don't want to."

"That's just it. I do want to. But it's—" she glanced his way "—difficult."

He was tempted to reach for her but got the feeling that wasn't the best idea. So he sipped his drink—which wasn't bad—and waited for her to continue.

"You probably remember me mentioning that I jogged with a friend every morning."

He nodded.

"One day, she called after I'd already arrived at the park to let me know she wasn't feeling well and wouldn't be able to make it. So I decided to jog anyway. Alone."

That last word coupled with the pained look on her face began to paint a grotesque picture in Gabriel's mind, but he remained silent.

"I was almost finished when someone came up behind me. He dragged me off the path." Her gaze was fixed on Aggie, and her petting became more vigorous. "I was so ashamed. Then, about the time I felt as though I might finally be coming up for air, I learned I was pregnant."

His eyes closed as he tried to process not only the physical, but mental agony plaguing her. Looking at her again, compassion and regret warred within him. "I'm so sorry, Jillian. Not only for what you've been through, but for thinking the worst about you. I know better than that." But his heart had told him he was the victim.

He kept his voice low as he encouraged her to look at him. "You have no reason to be ashamed."

"Everyone says that. But being violated isn't something that's easy to admit because you're constantly second-guessing yourself, wondering what you did or could have done differently. Like if I'd opted *not* to jog alone." She stared into her cup. "That's why I couldn't talk to you. I was too embarrassed."

Gabriel ached for the woman he'd come to care about and longed to find a way to fix it. That's what he did. Whenever someone faced a crisis, he rallied the troops and stepped in to do whatever needed to be done.

But what Jillian had suffered couldn't be fixed. She needed healing. The kind of healing only God could bring. And, maybe, someone to lean on when things got tough. A friend she could count on. Like him.

Moving his cup aside, he rested his arms on the table. "What made you decide to move to Hope Crossing?"

"Everyone knows everyone here. They watch out for each other. For as long as I can remember, whenever I'd come to visit Grandmama, people called her by name." A wistful look softened her expression. "When I was little, I thought maybe she was a celebrity or something. Then I grew to understand that's just how life was in Hope Crossing. So when Grandmama informed me that Rita Douglas was stepping down as library director…" She shrugged. "I don't believe the timing of that was a coincidence."

"No, I don't either. But then, I don't believe in coincidence."

The corners of her mouth lifted a notch. "This job gave me the opportunity to raise my baby in this idyllic place where people look out for one another."

"Wait." He gave his head a shake, wondering if he'd heard her correctly. "You're going to keep the baby?" He'd assumed she'd put it up for adoption.

Disappointment swam in her blue eyes, suggesting he wasn't the first to ask that question.

She pushed to her feet and began to pace, her slippers scuffing against the worn wooden floor.

Aggie did, too, keeping step with Jillian.

Arms wound tightly around her midsection, she said, "I don't expect you to understand, Gabriel. Most people can't."

"Jillian…" He stood and started to reach for her, then thought better of it. "Just because I don't understand doesn't mean I won't support you. I was taken aback, that's all. Choosing to keep a stranger's baby, well, that takes a lot of guts. I admire you."

Pausing, she nodded. "I appreciate that. I mean, this certainly isn't how I envisioned becoming a mother. But God doesn't always work things out the way we expect. What He does promise, though, is to work all things together for good to those who love Him. That's what I'm clinging to, regardless of what anyone else thinks."

"As it should be." Meaning he needed to stop dwelling on what might have been and focus on being the friend she needed now.

Realizing it hadn't thundered in a while, Gabriel moved to the door, shoved the peach-colored curtain out of the way and peered outside. "Looks like the storm has passed." Sadly, Jillian was still caught in the throes of a different kind of storm.

He turned to face her. "I should go. We both need some rest." And he needed to process. His gaze fell to Aggie sitting at Jillian's feet. "I think she likes you."

Jillian gave the dog a rub. "I'm growing rather fond of her, too."

He opened the door. "Aggie, come."

But the dog remained at Jillian's side. Because whether she knew it or not, Jillian needed Aggie.

"How would you feel about letting her stay here tonight? She's housebroken and generally sleeps through the night, so I don't foresee her keeping you awake."

Jillian scratched Aggie's head. "I don't know. What do you think, Aggie? Do you want to stay with me?"

The dog lay down on top of Jillian's slipper-covered feet.

Gabriel smiled. "I think you have your answer."

"Oh, but I have a doctor's appointment in Brenham at nine. I'm picking Grandmama up at eight so she can go with me."

"No problem. I'll retrieve Aggie before I leave for work in the morning."

"What time is that?"

"Around seven." Usually earlier, but she needed to rest. And with Aggie watching over her, he prayed Jillian would do just that.

Chapter Two

Jillian jolted out of a deep sleep, causing Aggie to groan at her side.

Shoving the hair out of her face, Jillian grappled in the darkness for her phone to stop the harp ringtone that was her alarm. Then she flopped onto her back.

"I don't want to get up." She hadn't slept that hard in months.

Then she remembered her doctor's appointment and that Gabriel would be picking up Aggie soon.

She swung her legs over the side of the too-firm full-size mattress and sat up to turn on the bedside lamp, squinting against the brightness. Still rubbing her eyes, she watched as Aggie leaped off the bed to stretch. Front, then back. Jillian couldn't help smiling. Doggy yoga.

Donning her robe, she shuffled into the kitchen,

where she turned on the fluorescent light over the sink and added a pod to her Keurig. One of the few items she'd brought with her from Dallas. Since Grandmama's place was fully furnished, Jillian wanted to go through everything before having her own furnishings brought down. A mission that would begin later today when she returned from Brenham.

She glanced down to find Aggie sitting at her side, peering up at her with those dark, soulful eyes. "Thank you for staying with me last night." Could that have been why Jillian had slept so well?

"I guess you need to go outside, don't you?"

Aggie darted toward the door.

Following her, Jillian turned on the porch light and nudged the curtain out of the way to peer outside. Across the drive the lights shone inside Milly's mirror-image home, letting Jillian know Gabriel was also awake.

Again, she looked down at the dog, who was waiting patiently. "I'd better let you take care of business before Gabriel has to leave." She unlocked and opened the wooden door before unlatching and pushing open the screen.

Aggie raced outside into the crisp morning air and was sniffing about when Gabriel emerged from his house in his usual work attire, jeans and a polo shirt.

Jillian pushed the screen door wider as he continued across the drive, a weary smile on his handsome face.

"Good, you're awake," he said. "That is, assuming you actually slept."

"Yes, I did. Surprisingly well, I might add."

He gave a nod of approval. "Glad to hear it."

"Now I need to fuel myself with some coffee—decaf, of course—and get ready for my appointment."

He cocked his head, concern creasing his brow. "Is the baby okay? You're not having any problems, are you?"

"No. This is just a routine check to establish a baseline with my new doctor."

"Ah. That's good."

Aggie trotted over to him and was rewarded with a scratch.

"You ready to go, girl?" He moved to his white vet truck—a standard pickup outfitted with a large insert in the bed, with lots of drawers and compartments to carry almost anything a veterinarian might need—and opened the door.

The dog hesitated, looking back at Jillian. Something that made her feel rather special.

"Go on, Aggie."

After a little more encouragement from Gabriel, the dog hopped into the cab.

Pausing, he looked Jillian's way. "Would you

be interested in going to the football game tonight? It's Hope Crossing's homecoming."

She couldn't help the sudden flutter in her heart. Was Gabriel asking her on a date?

"Most of the town will be there. Thought it might be a good opportunity for you to meet some folks."

Her cheeks heated as an annoying sense of disappointment snaked its way through her, twisting her insides. She and Gabriel were friends, nothing more. That's all they would ever be. She wasn't the same woman he'd held close while they'd danced. Or kissed beneath a full moon this past Valentine's Day.

"Maybe. Let's see how my day goes."

"I'll give you a call this afternoon." He waved as he climbed into his truck.

Watching him drive away, she took solace in the fact that she'd finally told him the truth. That seemingly insurmountable barrier that had stood between them for the past five months had been brought down, and she was grateful to call him a friend once again.

And with the grandmas expecting them to work together on the bazaar, that was definitely a good thing.

Back inside, she read a devotional while savoring her coffee and a kolache she'd picked up at

Plowman's yesterday. Then, after getting ready for her day, she went to collect Grandmama.

In recent months there'd been times when it felt as though she was the only one on Jillian's side, so it seemed appropriate Grandmama should accompany her to her appointment today. Jillian had purposely held off on learning the baby's gender until her grandmother was with her, and they were thrilled to find out she was having a girl. Though, they would have been just as happy with a boy. Too bad she couldn't say the same for her mother.

When they called to tell her, she said, "Oh, Jillian. I cannot tell you what a relief that is. I mean, a boy would have been nice, too, it just would have been more…challenging."

As if a boy would have been less worthy of their love?

Unwilling to allow her mother to squelch their happiness, Jillian and her grandmother celebrated with an early lunch at a cute little diner in downtown Brenham before stopping by the grocery store to pick up the order Jillian had placed online. On the way home, they discussed the bazaar and potential names for the baby.

When they returned to the senior-living community, Jillian accompanied her grandmother inside to share their secret with Milly. And when Jillian apologized for insisting Grandmama withhold the truth until now, Ms. Milly simply patted her hand, tears spilling onto her cheeks, and said, "That's all right, child. I've always been able to trust Ida Mae with my secrets, too." Then she added, "If there's anything I can do, anything at all, don't you hesitate to call me, you hear?" The woman's aged brown eyes bore into hers.

"Thank you, Ms. Milly." She turned her attention to her grandmother. "I hate to cut this short, but I need to get back to the house and take care of those groceries."

"I know you do." Grandmama eased into her chair. "Don't forget they're coming by to fill the propane tank this afternoon. Not that they'll need you for anything. They usually just leave the bill at the door."

Unfortunately, it meant having a stranger at the house. And while common sense told her the worker was probably an upstanding person, the jaded side of her gnawed at her resolve.

"Would you like me to go with you, Jilly?" Grandmama was onto her.

Jillian stiffened her spine. "I have to face my fears. However, if need be, I'll call you to chat."

Outside, she quickly scanned her surroundings before starting toward her vehicle. The early-afternoon air was warm, but at least the humidity was low. Hopefully that meant things would cool more efficiently once the sun set. Making it a perfect night for football.

Gabriel's parting words about calling her came to mind as she got into her car and started the engine. She'd better decide soon. Something that would be much easier if she hadn't jumped to conclusions this morning and sent her heart into a tizzy.

Less than five minutes later, she pulled into the drive at Grandmama's, her gaze darting between the two single-story Victorian homes that sat at the end of the street on the eastern edge of town, each with a large oak tree in the front yard and separated by two single-car gravel driveways. Both houses were painted a beautiful sage green and trimmed in white. Yet while Grandmama's front door was a dark blue-green, Milly's sported a deep red.

Jillian parked and did a quick perusal of the yards, the detached garages at the back of each drive sending her imagination into overdrive. She closed her eyes. *Lord, You are my strength and my shield. I will trust in You.*

Drawing in a deep breath, she stepped out of her car. She clutched her keys as she climbed the trio of steps at the side of the house, then continued straight ahead to the kitchen door. The wooden screen creaked when she opened it. After turning the key in the lock, she took another breath and stepped inside to move from room to room, checking closets and under beds. Perhaps she was being ridiculous, but she would never again take her safety for granted. Even in Hope Crossing.

Convinced all was well, she went back outside to retrieve her groceries. Soon, the chipped laminate butcher-block counters were littered with plastic bags. Since all she'd brought from her former kitchen was an array of spices and a few canned goods, she had a freezer, refrigerator and pantry to stock.

After putting away the cold and frozen items, she set to work wrapping some boneless chicken breasts individually in foil. Until a knock on the kitchen door had her stiffening. Her gaze jerked to the door, but the curtain over the window obstructed her view. She darted a glance to the window left of the door where, between the valance and curtain tier, she spotted Gabriel's truck.

Setting the fork on the counter beside the chicken, she moved to the door to greet him. "Hi."

With Aggie at his side, he eyed her suspiciously. "Everything all right?"

She brushed her hair away from her face. "It will be, just as soon as this heart-pounding panic that seizes me every time I have an unexpected visitor subsides."

"I'm sorry." Compassion lined his brow. "From now on I'll call or text, so you'll know to expect me."

How could she not smile at this kindhearted man? "You don't have to do that."

"If it helps keep you calm, I will. Your being stressed isn't good for the baby. Which reminds me, how'd your appointment go?"

She pushed the screen open and motioned for him to come inside. "Good. Routine. And we learned the gender of the baby."

When she paused, he said, "Don't keep me hanging."

Inexplicable joy welled inside of her. "It's a girl."

His smile seemed to outshine her own. "Congratulations!"

"Thank you. I'm excited, though it wouldn't have mattered either way." She smoothed a hand over her stomach. "I love this little one no matter what."

"I know you do."

"So what brings you by? I thought you'd be at the clinic."

"I'm on my way back there now. I had to visit a pregnant mare. But I thought I'd see if you were home. Aggie gets kind of bored hanging around the clinic." He shrugged. "Thought I'd see if you'd mind keeping her company."

"Me keep her company? How about the other way around? Of course she can stay."

"And there's one other reason."

His hesitation had her biting her bottom lip. "Which is?"

"Have you made a decision about the homecoming game?"

She supposed it would be good to meet some more people. Especially since she'd be running the library. Getting to know one's patrons was always a good idea. But spending so much time with Gabriel could be detrimental to her heart. Make her long for the way things used to be.

But she should get out of the house, too. The fresh air would do her good.

"I understand if you're busy," he said.

She gave herself a shake. "No, I'm not that busy." With a deep breath, she said, "Actually, I think it would be fun. Thank you for inviting me." Now she just needed to keep reminding herself that this was not a date and they were only friends.

Friday-night lights. Gabriel had been to almost every Hope Crossing home game for as long as he could remember, save for his time at A&M when he'd traded most Friday nights for Saturdays at Kyle Field. But even that couldn't compare to small-town football, where no matter what differences you might have with other folks, you came together under a single banner to cheer your team on to victory. And on homecoming night, even those who weren't fans of the sport came out to mingle with former classmates who'd returned for the event. Making it a perfect opportunity for Jillian to meet a lot of people.

"Are you going to be warm enough?" Crossing the parking lot toward the stadium, holding onto Aggie's leash, he glanced at Jillian keeping pace beside him in her skinny jeans and a white T-shirt topped with a lightweight khaki cardigan.

"Yes. Though, since I have yet to unpack, I had to make do." She looked around him to Aggie. "How come she's wearing a service vest?"

"For her safety. And so people are less likely to balk about someone bringing a dog to the game." He was also testing out a theory. The way Aggie had behaved at Jillian's last night, refusing to leave with him, suggested she sensed something in Jillian. A need that Aggie could aid Jillian with, the way she had her former handler.

It still pained Gabriel when he thought about the terror-filled look in Jillian's pretty blue eyes last night. He hated seeing her that way. The fact that one random act of violence had taken so much from this once-vivacious woman gutted him. And he'd been bending God's ear about it all day, asking why bad things happened to good people.

Now Gabriel was determined to do whatever he could to help Jillian fight back and reclaim her confidence. And, perhaps, helping her integrate into the community would aid that process. Make her feel more comfortable in her new surroundings.

They purchased their tickets at the gate before proceeding past the tall chain-link fence into Hawks Stadium. Rock music blared from speakers at one end of the field as the two teams warmed up, while the aroma of fresh popcorn drifted from the concession stand, igniting his appetite.

Pausing beside the bleachers, he leaned toward Jillian. "Do you want to grab food now or later?"

"We could start with some popcorn and go from there."

He smiled down at her. "You can't resist the smell either, can you?"

"Never." She paused, her eyes widening as she looked past him. "Wow! That is the biggest mum I have ever seen."

Turning, he spotted a young man sporting a mum-topped garter around his bicep with ribbons and charms in the school colors dangling from it. But that was nothing compared to his date's. The poor girl's mum was almost as big as she was. It hung around her neck and sported at least four white mums, lights and a white teddy bear while an overabundance of blue and white ribbons, boas and beads hung all the way to her feet.

He released a low whistle. “Takes some core strength to stand straight with that one.”

“I’ve never seen anything like it.” Jillian shook her head. “I mean, mums were a big deal when I was in school, but that’s over-the-top. Can you imagine what he must’ve paid for that?”

Gabriel shook his head. Only one of many reasons why he’d never asked a girl to homecoming.

“C’mon, let’s get that popcorn.”

Once they’d procured their snack and a couple bottles of water, they started through the rapidly growing crowd in search of seats.

“Jillian!”

Nearing the bleachers once again, they both turned in the direction of the female voice to see Annalise Prescott hurrying toward them while her husband, Hawkins, trailed behind, holding two-year-old Olivia, Annalise’s daughter with her late husband, who Hawkins had adopted.

Gabriel couldn’t help noticing the way Jillian’s face lit up at the sight of her friend. Annalise, who owned the Hope Crossing Christmas Tree Farm, had moved to Hope Crossing from Dallas a little over a year ago, and the two women had struck up a conversation at the tree farm last December. Then, when Hawkins and Annalise wed this past April, Jillian had been Gabriel's date. It was one of the best nights of his life, ending with an incredible kiss that had left him with high hopes for their future, never guessing they'd be shattered only weeks later.

The two women embraced while Gabriel and Hawkins shook hands.

When the women parted, Annalise said, "I didn't think you were coming until tomorrow."

"No, I arrived yesterday."

Giving Jillian a visual once-over, a seemingly nonplussed Annalise said, "You look great. How are you feeling?"

"Good."

The exchange had Gabriel wondering if Jillian had confided in Annalise about her pregnancy. Whatever the case, she seemed relaxed.

"Doggy." Tucked in Hawkins's arms, Olivia peered down at Aggie.

"That's right," his friend said. "But that's a special doggy. That vest she's wearing means she can't play right now."

The little blonde looked to Gabriel, as if to confirm what her father said was correct. Then she scrunched her little nose and grinned.

"Where are y'all sitting?" Annalise looked from Jillian to Gabriel.

"We haven't made it that far yet," he said.

"Mind if we join you, then?" asked Annalise.

Jillian deferred to Gabriel.

"Not at all." He pointed toward the crowded walkway. "Lead the way."

Soon they settled in midway up the bleachers, just this side of the fifty-yard line. Annalise slid in next to her husband, Jillian beside her, then Gabriel took the end and Aggie sat between them at their feet.

The two women continued to chat, eyeing every mum that passed, occasionally shaking their heads. Jillian rubbed Aggie every once in a while, and Gabriel sensed she was relaxing. He was glad they'd run into Hawkins and Annalise. The more people Jillian knew, the more comfortable she'd feel.

Several minutes and half a bag of popcorn later, Jillian nudged him with her elbow. "Sorry, I don't mean to ignore you."

"Don't worry about me." He was curious, though. Turning so his mouth was close to her ear, he breathed in her sweet fragrance. "Does Annalise know?"

Jillian shook her head before leaning his way. "I called her about childcare before I accepted the position. I didn't offer any details, though, and she didn't ask."

He smiled then. "That's the mark of a good friend."

Pink crept into her cheeks. "I hope she doesn't think you're responsible. I mean, we were…" Her gaze drifted away.

"Dating?"

She nodded.

"We know the truth, and so does God. No one else matters."

The noise level in the small stadium rose significantly when the band started to play the school song and the team raced onto the field. After the homecoming king and queen were announced, the national anthem was played, and the game was underway.

A third of the way into the second quarter, Gabriel leaned toward Jillian. "I need something more substantial than popcorn. Can I bring you something, or would you prefer to come with me?"

"I'll come with you."

He stepped out with Aggie in tow, allowing Jillian to go in front of him.

Though the concession stand wasn't that far away, all the people stopping him to say hello or shake hands made the short trek take longer.

"Hey, Gabriel." At the far end of the first row, Jake Walker waved with his free hand while the other held tightly to that of his wife, Alli.

Since it was rare to see them without their

four-year-old daughter and three-year-old son, Gabriel said, "What? No kids?"

"They're with my mom," said Jake.

Gabriel looked Jillian's way. "These two are yet another reason why my Sunday-school class keeps shrinking." Three couples had married in the last year and transitioned from the single-adult class to the young-marrieds.

He returned his attention to Jake and Alli. "Do y'all remember Jillian?" She'd been a frequent visitor prior to May.

"I do." Alli peered up at her, her brow pinched. "Are you the new library director?"

Jillian smiled. "Yes, I start Monday."

"We spoke on the phone." The other woman stood. "I'm Alli. We spoke about a childcare reservation."

Jillian smiled. "You're the director at the early learning center."

"That's me. I actually have it on my calendar to call you in the next week or two."

Suddenly Jillian looked concerned. "Oh?"

"Not about childcare," Alli assured. "Regarding the library. Children's Story Hour, in particular."

Now standing beside his wife, Jake poked a thumb her way. "Alli is the one who does the reading. And let me tell you, she's got a real gift."

"Yeah, yeah." Alli elbowed him.

"Actually, Rita mentioned you during our interview, though I never put two and two together until now. Is this a weekly event?"

"Only once a month. However, I'd like it to be more often. Since I work full-time, I'm only available on Saturdays. Perhaps we could discuss bumping it to twice a month."

"I don't see why not. Though, I'll know better once I actually start my new position and get settled in."

"I'll try to stop in one day. Maybe the week after next."

"I'll look forward to it."

"You're definitely not a stranger around here." Gabriel held tight to Aggie's leash as they walked away.

"That's a good thing, I guess. Because there are times when I'm not even sure who I am anymore."

Jillian's comment tugged at his heart. And while he wanted to find out why, standing in the concession line surrounded by a bunch of people wasn't the right place.

By the time they made it to the counter, there was only a minute remaining in the quarter. They each ordered a hot dog and nachos, though the candy for dessert was a last-minute addition.

When they finally started back to their seats, the halftime show had begun, and they were like two salmon swimming upstream. People crowded the narrow walkway, bumping into one another, and Gabriel feared someone might step on Aggie's paws. But a quick glance at the canine proved the dog was holding her own.

When they finally made it to their seats, Gabriel stood aside and waited for Jillian to go in ahead of him. But she wasn't there. He'd thought she was right behind him.

He surveyed the stream of people shuffling along the walkway. That's when he saw her. Seemingly lost in the crowd, standing frozen, her arms wrapped around her midsection, her stare glassy, her face pale.

Knowing he had to get to her, he hastily deposited the cardboard tray of food beneath his seat. When he straightened again, someone bumped into his shoulder as they passed. With all these people, he couldn't get to Jillian fast enough.

Unhooking Aggie's leash, he said, "Aggie, find Jillian."

The dog immediately left his side, and Gabriel could only pray she'd meet with success.

He watched as the poodle nimbly maneuvered down the bleachers and around people until she reached Jillian's side. And he could tell the exact moment Jillian became aware of the dog's presence. Her pinched expression relaxed, and her slumped shoulders lifted slightly.

And as she seemed to search him out, Gabriel made his way to her as quickly as he could, chastising himself for not paying closer attention. He should've been behind her, not in front of her. Should've held on to her hand and made sure she felt safe.

As he neared Jillian, he noticed her white-knuckle grip on the handle of Aggie's vest. Then their gazes connected, and she visibly relaxed.

The reaction made his heart swell and strengthened his resolve to do whatever it took to help her rediscover the confident woman she'd once been.

Chapter Three

Jillian awoke before dawn the next morning, embarrassment over last night's panic attack still haunting her. Poor Gabriel. She doubted he'd be extending her any more invitations. Because instead of enjoying the game, he'd ended up playing babysitter to her. And regret had paired with anxiety to keep her awake most of the night. So much so that she'd allowed herself one cup of caffeinated coffee this morning. Between that and a shower, she was now ready to get started on her day.

Other than her groceries and a load of laundry, she hadn't made much progress yesterday. So since tomorrow was church and Monday the first day of her new job, clothing was her first order of business today. But before she could get her things put away, she had to make room. Grandmama's closets and drawers were still full of stuff, making Jillian wonder what she'd taken with her.

Now to figure out what to do with the clothes her grandmother left behind.

Taking her phone from the pocket of her jeans, she dialed Grandmama just after eight.

"Mornin', Jilly."

"Good morning, Grandmama."

"How was the game?"

With zero desire to relive her mortification, she said, "Good. Hope Crossing won."

"Wonderful. What's on your agenda for today?"

"Getting settled. Which is why I'm calling. Grandmama, you have *way* too many clothes."

A hearty chuckle echoed through the line. "Only because I never got rid of anything. Thanks to the Great Depression, I was raised to make the most out of what I had. Clothes could be passed down or the fabric cut up for quilts."

"Grandmama, when did you ever make a quilt?"

"I didn't. But I'd have had plenty of fabric to do so if I'da wanted to." The woman cackled.

"I'll say." Jillian pulled a hanger from the closet and eyed the bell-bottom pants. "And when was the last time you wore bell-bottoms?"

"Never. Those belonged to your mother."

Jillian shook her head. "If she hasn't claimed them by now, then I say good riddance."

"Since I can't remember even a quarter of what's still there, you may as well get rid of all of it. That is, unless you think it's something sentimental, like my wedding dress."

When Jillian was a little girl, Grandmama used to let her try on her wedding dress. Jillian still remembered staring at her reflection, wondering what it would feel like to be a bride. Like a princess for a day as she wed her Prince Charming.

Shaking off the memory, along with any notions of finding her prince, she said, "Don't worry. If I question anything, I will let you know."

She'd just ended the call when a text came in from Gabriel.

I can't put Aggie off anymore. She's headed your way.

Jillian moved from the middle bedroom, across the center hall and into the kitchen. For as embarrassed as she was about last night, she was also grateful Gabriel had brought Aggie to the game. If it hadn't been for her, there was no telling how long Jillian would've stood there in a state of panic. All because people were pressing in around her and she felt trapped.

Until Aggie had nudged her hand, bringing Jillian to her senses.

Gabriel had even suggested Aggie remain with her again last night, but Jillian felt bad about doing that. Aggie was his dog, after all.

She tugged open the kitchen door as Aggie bounded up the steps. The cool morning air whisked over Jillian's skin as she pushed open the screen. "Good morning."

The dog readily entered, her docked tail wagging while she danced around Jillian.

Her gaze again moved outside as Gabriel eased up the steps wearing faded jeans and a maroon Texas A&M T-shirt. His hair was still damp as though he'd just showered. And his smile? All she had to say about that was she was getting irritated at the way her heart stuttered every time she saw him. They were no longer a couple—that is, if they ever had been—nor would they ever be. She was damaged goods. End of story.

Now, if she could only get her heart to fall in line.

"How'd you sleep?" He stepped inside, a travel mug in hand.

"Not too bad." Not too good either, but he didn't need to know that. "What are your plans for this beautiful Saturday?" She immediately wished she could snatch the words back. He probably thought she wanted him to hang around here with her.

"I put the finishing touches on my Sunday-school lesson this morning, so I'm going to make a run to Brenham for some groceries." He rubbed the stubble lining his jaw and chin, giving him a rugged appearance. "How about you?"

"My plan is to make a concerted effort to settle in here. Unpack. Freshen things up. I'm glad it's cooler today." She shrugged. "Who knows? Maybe I'll be able to open a few windows." If she could convince herself it was safe.

"It's not too bad out there now, but it's supposed to get pretty breezy this afternoon."

Nodding, she rocked back on the heels of her slip-on sneakers, feeling suddenly awkward. She slid her hands into the back pockets of her jeans and sucked in a breath. "Thank you again for inviting me to the game. I'm sorry I ruined things."

"Ruined? What are you talking about? Hope Crossing won."

She cut a glance his way. "You know what I mean."

Moving closer, he said, "Jillian, if anyone should be sorry, it's me."

"You? What did you do?"

He shook his head. "It's not what I did, but what I didn't do. I should've been more conscientious and stayed with you."

"I'm a grown woman. I shouldn't need a babysitter."

"Stop being so hard on yourself. We're friends. Friends stick by each other."

Always the good guy. A friend to all. That was Gabriel. She only wished she wasn't so needy.

Her phone dinged, and she retrieved it from the table. A message from Annalise.

Are you home? I have something to bring you.

Jillian moved her thumbs across the screen.

Yes. I can't wait.

She smiled, slipping the phone into her back pocket. "Annalise is on her way over."

"That's great," he said.

Yes, now he wouldn't feel the need to keep an eye on her.

"I'll get out of your hair, then." He pushed the screen open. "Aggie. Come."

The dog sat at Jillian's feet and stared at him, making Jillian smile. "Since you're going shopping, she's welcome to stay with me."

Something in his expression seemed to relax. "You're sure?"

"She can keep me company while I clean."

Gabriel agreed, then went back to his house,

and a short time later, his maroon F-150 pulled out of his drive.

No sooner had he left when a blue SUV eased into her driveway. Moments later, Annalise bounded up the steps, carrying a cardboard box.

Jillian hurried to open the door. "Oh my. What have you got there?"

"Just call me the Welcome Wagon." Her friend stepped inside to set the box on the table.

"Whatever you've got in there smells delicious." Jillian inhaled the enticing aromas.

"Chicken spaghetti, some pumpkin muffins and chocolate chip cookies."

"Mmm. I can hardly wait till lunchtime."

Annalise perched a hand on her hip. "How are you doing? You seemed a little, I don't know, troubled last night."

Jillian's cheeks heated. "I'm much better today, thank you." She couldn't help feeling as though she owed Annalise some sort of explanation.

Aggie nudged Jillian's hand, so she indulged her canine friend. "Without getting into any details, my pregnancy probably isn't what you're thinking."

"I *think* you're having a baby."

Jillian smiled then. "That part is correct. What I was referring to is how I ended up this way."

"Which is none of my business."

Jillian appreciated Annalise's understanding. "I can tell you that I'm having a little girl, though."

Her friend's face lit up. "Oh, little girls are so much fun. Not that I've had any experience with little boys. At least not yet." She paused. "Now, about the Christmas Bazaar."

"Yes?" They had discussed it last night.

"The tree farm would like to donate one seven-foot tree of the purchaser's choosing."

"That'll be a hit."

"We're also throwing in lights, ornaments and a stand, which we'll drop off at the church. Then the purchaser will simply come to the tree farm with their certificate—which I will get to you later—to pick out their tree."

"Annalise, that's perfect. Not only do they get the Christmas tree, they get to enjoy the whole experience of the hunt, cutting it down and decorating it. Thank you so much. The grandmas are going to be tickled pink."

"Speaking of grandmas—" Annalise glanced from the kitchen into the dining room "—cute house."

Jillian surveyed the home she'd visited all her life. "I've always thought so. It could use some serious updating, though." With Aggie on her heels, she rounded the table to move through the doorway into the dining room on her way to the living room, motioning for Annalise to follow. "Take a look at this."

Annalise joined her in the large opening separating the living and dining rooms. "Oh my." Eyes wide, she took in the sponged pale-peach walls, ruffled floral sofa and peach carpet. "Talk about lost in the 1990s." She eyed the mirrored Victorian fireplace surround to their right. "I'm glad she refrained from painting that. It's gorgeous."

"Agreed." Jillian's gaze fell to the floor. "I can't say the same for this carpet."

"I see what you mean." Annalise glanced her way. "On the bright side, there's probably wood underneath it, so depending on what shape that's in, it could be an easy fix. I'm sure you could get Gabriel to help you. He's a handy fellow to have around." Her friend smiled. "You may not know this, but only weeks before the Christmas-tree farm was due to open last year, a storm destroyed my barn. The next day, Gabriel showed up with other members of our Sunday-school class to help with the cleanup. And then they were back days later to help with the rebuilding. It was pretty amazing."

"Sounds like it." And yet another reason why she shouldn't read anything into Gabriel's actions.

Annalise started toward the kitchen again. "I

need to get back to the house. Everything around the tree farm has to be cleaned and decorated before Thanksgiving so we're ready to open the day after."

"Thank you for the food, not to mention your suggestions for the living room. You've inspired me."

Annalise stepped outside, the wind tossing her blond hair. "Glad I could help."

Energized, Jillian tucked the casserole into the refrigerator, pushed up the sleeves of her sweatshirt and returned to the bedroom to continue clearing and unpacking, pausing only long enough to respond to Gabriel's text message asking if she wanted something from Whataburger. The entire time, her mind raced with ideas for transforming Grandmama's house. Of course, she'd have to check with Grandmama first.

By noon, Jillian had filled two trash bags with items that weren't worth donating, all of her clothes had been put away and she was eager to move on to the next task. Yet, while there were many things to be done, the living room kept calling to her.

After dropping the last trash bag by the back door, she again made her way into the living room, cringing as her gaze fell to the carpet. Aside from the kitchen, this was the room where she and her baby would spend most of their time.

Thoughts of her little girl sparked a sense of urgency. If Jillian didn't get things done before she had the baby, she'd be so busy she might never accomplish them. Meaning she needed to start tackling them now. But with the bazaar and her new job, when would she find the time?

Movement outside the window set her heart to pounding.

Then she realized it was only Gabriel's truck pulling into the drive. She promptly chastised herself while Aggie nudged her hand. Wasn't it bad enough that she'd made a fool of herself in public last night? Why did every little thing send her into a panic? It was as if the woman she'd once been had never existed. And as she moved through the dining room toward the kitchen, she wished she could find her way back to that woman. Not only for her sake, but for her child's.

"You're awfully quiet." At Jillian's kitchen table, Gabriel set his patty melt atop its wrapper and grabbed another onion ring, observing the woman beside him as she twirled a fry through ketchup. "Everything all right?"

With a shrug, she plunged the fry into her mouth and nodded. "Just pondering."

"What are you pondering?" After devouring the onion ring, he reached for his Dr Pepper.

She didn't respond. Instead, she took a long

draw on her strawberry milkshake, then heaved a sigh as she set it back on the table. "I've always loved this house. But now that I'm living here, I think I'd like to make some changes."

"Such as?" He took a drink.

She pointed to the doorway between the kitchen and dining room. "Have you seen that living room?"

He couldn't help but laugh. "Oh, yes. Mamaw's was almost identical before I brought it into the twenty-first century." He stuffed the last bite of burger into his mouth.

"Do you know if there are wood floors beneath that atrocious carpet?"

Nodding, he wiped his hands on a napkin. "Considering the kitchen and hallway have them, and that they ran throughout my grandmother's place, I assume there are. The bigger question is what shape are they in?"

"How do we find out?"

"You'll have to lift the carpet."

Mischief sparked in her blue eyes, granting him a glimpse of the old Jillian. "Or I could get someone to do it for me."

"Sure." He eyed the empty sandwich wrapper in front of her. "Are you finished?"

Taking hold of her milkshake, she stood.

He tossed their trash before following her from the practical kitchen, through the fussy dining room into the flowery living room that almost mirrored Mamaw's, prior to the overhaul he'd done a couple of years ago.

While Jillian paused beside the ruffled floral sofa, Aggie at her side, he looked for an inconspicuous spot. "I could start in this corner over here." He pointed to a section left of the opening between the living and dining rooms.

"That should be fine."

Retrieving a pocketknife from his jeans, he knelt to pry the edge of the carpet away from the tack strip. "This rug has definitely seen better days."

"I know. All that ground-in dirt. Makes me shudder when I think about my baby crawling on it."

He dug the blade of the knife under the padding. "At least you've got some time before that'll happen." Setting the knife aside, he grabbed hold of the carpet and pad and peeled it as far away from the wall as he could, letting go a low whistle. "Man, that's some pretty wood." He glanced over his shoulder. "Vintage longleaf pine, just like my house."

She looked over his shoulder. "That is pretty. Why would anyone cover that up?"

"It was the trendy thing to do."

Biting her bottom lip, she scanned the rest of the space. "That's just one corner. What do you suppose the rest of it looks like?"

"The only way to find out is to peel back enough to expose the high-traffic areas. And I can't do that without cutting the carpet."

She frowned. "I'll need to check with Grandmama on that. I mean, even though she'll never live here again, it's still her house."

He let the carpet fall back into place and stood to face her. "For what it's worth, Mamaw gave me permission to do whatever I wanted with her house. Within reason, of course. I suspect Ms. Ida Mae will extend you the same courtesy. I mean, you're only talking about cosmetic changes, right?"

"Yes. The whole house needs to be painted, but I can do that myself."

"I don't think so."

She sent him an indignant look. "Excuse me?"

"You're pregnant. You have no business on a ladder."

Arms crossed over her chest, she scowled. "Then, do you know of someone I can hire to do it for me?"

"Why? Painting's easy. I can do it."

She squared her shoulders. "I'll pay you, then."

"No, you won't."

"Why not?"

"Because I offer—" The sound of glass shattering echoed from somewhere inside the house.

While it had startled him, Jillian froze, the

color draining from her face. "What. Was. That?" The words came out on jerky breaths.

He eased beside her. "Sounded like a window."

Her fingers gripped his forearm, nails digging into his skin, while her entire body trembled. "What if someone is trying to get in?"

He doubted that. Especially since it was early afternoon. But trying to convince Jillian wasn't going to be easy.

"I'm sure there's a logical explanation, but I need to go investigate. Do you want to come with me or stay here with Aggie?" Who was practically attached to Jillian's side.

"I—I don't know." She looked up at him, her blue eyes wide.

Prying her fingers from his arm, he kept hold of her hands. "Listen to me, Jillian. I'm not going to let anything happen to you."

She nodded in rapid succession. "Okay." Pulling one hand away, she gave in to Aggie's urging and petted the dog. "I'll go with you."

Still holding Jillian's hand, he led her into the center hall. "It sounded as though it came from the back of the house." Ignoring the bedroom opposite the living room, he moved farther into the house.

Everything appeared to be in order in the middle bedroom.

The bathroom was next, but it was intact.

The smell of fresh air touched his nostrils as they approached the final bedroom. "Do you have a window open in there?"

Jillian shook her head.

A window had definitely broken, but what had caused it remained a mystery.

He pointed toward the room. "Aggie, search."

Jillian's grip on him tightened when the poodle disappeared into the room. "She can do that?"

"And a whole lot more."

"What about the glass?"

"Don't worry. She's a trained professional."

Moments later, the dog returned without having made a sound.

Gabriel looked at Jillian. "If she'd sensed anyone in there, she would've barked."

"So it's good that she didn't?" She continued to quiver.

"Yes." He peered around the corner to see glass shards scattered about the small room with windows on two walls and the tip of a large tree limb sticking through one of the windows at the far end, while the wind tossed the lacy curtains about. "As I suspected." He urged Jillian into the doorway so she could see for herself.

"How did that happen?" Her eyes were still wide.

"Let's go outside and have a look."

Once they were on the porch, he stepped in

front of her while Aggie remained at Jillian's side. "I want you to take a couple of deep breaths for me."

She complied, her ponytail dancing in the breeze. "I'm sorry. I have a habit of overreacting these days."

"I understand. For what it's worth, it startled me, too."

She sent him a tremulous smile.

When they finally made it to the other side of the house, they saw that a limb had broken away from a dead tree. Probably from the wind.

Gabriel dragged his fingers through his hair. "Looks like I'm going to have to take the blame for this one. Every time I mow I tell myself that tree needs to come down. And then I forget about it." He looked at her now. "Sorry about that."

"At least there's a logical explanation." She was still shaky, though. "What do we do about the window?"

"For now, I'll need to cover it. Then we'll get a glass repairperson out here next week. Thankfully, I have a sheet of plywood in my garage, so I can get it covered. And before you start worrying, I'll be attaching it with screws, so the house will be secure."

The rigid set of her shoulders relaxed another notch. "Thank you for understanding."

Once he'd gathered everything he needed, he

donned a pair of gloves and quickly removed the debris from the opening, along with any precarious bits of glass, before securing the wood to the framing with the help of his cordless drill.

Despite the stout wind, Jillian watched him the entire time, her hair whipping about as she repeatedly petted Aggie, who had yet to budge from her side.

Finally, he stepped off the ladder. "I think we're all set."

"Thank you." Jillian kept a hand on Aggie. "How about I reward you with your choice of the pumpkin muffins or cookies Annalise brought?"

"You mean I have to choose?"

That seemed to make her smile as they started around to the other side of the house, passing beneath a majestic oak.

When they neared the porch, Aggie rushed to his F-150.

"Sorry, girl. We're not going anywhere."

Standing on her hind legs, she pawed at the door.

"What is it?"

To his surprise, the dog barked.

"Wait," he said, "I know what the problem is." Setting his drill and the screws on the steps, he looked at Jillian. "Her ball is in the truck."

While Jillian continued onto the porch, Gabriel opened the door for Aggie, who hopped into the cab. Except she didn't go for the ball he kept in the cup holder. Instead, she retrieved something from the back seat.

When she rejoined him, he realized she had her red service vest clutched in her mouth.

"What are you doing with that?"

The dog looked from him to Jillian and back.

"Well, I'll be." Gabriel knelt in front of the dog and took the rolled-up vest from her. "You're ready to get back to work, aren't you?" He'd suspected Jillian could benefit from Aggie's help. Obviously Aggie concurred.

The dog panted, waiting.

"And you want to help Jillian." He rubbed the dog's head. "We'll have to see what she says about that."

Aggie nudged the vest with her nose. "Okay, hold on." After unrolling it, he clipped it onto Aggie.

Gabriel had never seen the dog more eager. "All right, girl, let's go see what Jillian has to say about your offer."

Aggie rushed toward the porch where Jillian waited, arms crossed as though holding herself together.

"What's going on?" She sent Gabriel a curious look as he neared.

"Well," he said, topping the steps, "it appears Aggie has decided you're her new handler."

Confusion creased Jillian's brow as Aggie moved beside her. "I don't understand."

"You know how I said she belonged to one of my clients?"

She nodded.

"Aggie wasn't just his pet. She was his service dog. He suffered from PTSD, so Aggie would help him, whether he needed comfort or protection or assistance. She could sense when he was having or about to have a panic attack and distract him by providing tactile stimulation."

"Like the way she either licks my hand or urges me to pet her?"

"Exactly. And it appears Aggie isn't ready to retire. She wants to help you."

"What does that mean?"

He shrugged. "She wants to be your dog. To live with you. Go to work with you."

"Will they allow that?"

"She's a service dog. It's discrimination if they don't. They don't have to know what she's helping you with. But she does need to wear her vest. Her vest lets Aggie as well as other people know that she's working."

"I—I don't know what to say."

"You'll need some instruction on what to expect and how you and she will work together, but I think she could be a great asset to you. Your panic attacks, in particular. So what do you say?"

Jillian knelt beside the dog. "Like you, I don't believe in coincidence." She cupped Aggie's chin. "I think God brought the two of us together for a reason. So, Aggie, if you're set on helping me, who am I to say no?"

Standing again, Jillian peered up at him, looking almost bashful. "Thank you, Gabriel. For everything."

"My pleasure." Looking down at her, he knew he'd do almost anything to help her rediscover the vibrant woman she'd once been. "Now, why don't you call your grandmother about that carpet while I clean up the glass in the bedroom? Then we need to start making a list, because between turning this house into your home, coordinating the Christmas Bazaar and you starting a new job, we've got a lot to do."

Chapter Four

If there was one thing Jillian couldn't stand, it was a drama queen. Yet while her little sister, Alexandra, was the queen of drama queens, events since Jillian's arrival in Hope Crossing had her feeling as though the crown had been passed to her. Seemed every time she was with Gabriel she had some sort of meltdown. So why he'd asked her to join him on a trip to the home-improvement center in Brenham Sunday afternoon was beyond her.

But since Grandmama had given her blessing for Jillian to do whatever she wanted with the house, Jillian was eager to get the ball rolling. She'd love nothing more than to be settled by Christmas. To have the home improvements completed and her own furniture moved in. Though, what she was going to do with Grandmama's furniture was still a mystery. At a minimum, the sofa, side chairs and ottoman would need to go before Jillian could move her things in. They might be in good condition, but they were stuck in a time warp.

As the countryside whizzed past, she pondered the man in the driver's seat, while Aggie stretched out in the back seat. "That was a good Sunday-school lesson this morning."

"Thanks." He glanced her way. "Sometimes I feel as though God is directing the lessons right at me, and this was one of them."

She'd kind of felt that way, too. "Any particular part?"

"Not being forsaken by God. Not to be dismayed." He appeared to tighten his grip on the steering wheel. "It frustrates me that Doc won't retire. He keeps saying the practice is going to be mine, yet he refuses to release control. He insists on doing all the ordering and balks if I ask for something *he* thinks we don't need." He let go a sigh. "Sorry, I didn't mean to dump on you."

"How can you say that? I'm the one who came into town with a whole dump truck and dropped the load at your feet."

"And I'm glad you did. Because now I understand. When I heard you were moving into Ida Mae's house, I was prepared to hate you."

She lifted a brow. "Gabriel, I don't think you're capable of hating."

"Maybe, but I was definitely prepared to strongly dislike you."

That made her chuckle.

"It's good to hear you laugh, Jillian."

"It feels good."

"They don't say it's the best medicine for nothing, you know."

"Yes. My life has been way too serious in recent months."

"Understandable."

She reached into the back seat to give Aggie a rub. "Maybe now that Aggie has decided to be my companion, I'll be able to enjoy life a little more."

"I hope so." He stared straight ahead, his expression unreadable. Was he tired of having to deal with her? Did he feel as though he was stuck? Forced to look after her?

Her insides twisted, and she stared at her clasped hands in her lap as they approached the Brenham city limits. She needed to stop relying on Gabriel so much. They'd had their chance as a couple. But she'd been more interested in her career. They obviously weren't meant to be.

When they pulled into the home-improvement center parking lot a few minutes later, Jillian eagerly hopped out, Aggie following her. Taking hold of the dog's leash, Jillian tilted her face toward the cloudless sky and let the sun's warmth chase away the chill of the truck's air-conditioning.

"So what color are you thinking of?" Gabriel kept pace with her shorter strides as they started toward the entrance.

"Something greige."

"That narrows it down to only hundreds of choices. Light, medium or a darker shade?"

"Light to medium."

"More gray or beige?"

"I'm not certain. My furniture is a blue-gray, so I don't want too much gray."

The store's automatic doors slid open, and they continued inside.

"It's impossible to make a distinction in the store, though. You have to look at them in the room and see how the light reflects." Her steps slowed as they moved past the customer-service desk, and she couldn't help smiling. "They have Christmas stuff." The words came out in a singsong manner.

She'd always loved this time of year, when Christmas decorations began popping up everywhere. Meanwhile, she absolutely dreaded going into stores that last week before Christmas when the shelves grew bare or, even worse, Valentine's stuff started to appear.

"Do you have a need for a giant inflatable snow globe?"

She lifted her eyes to meet Gabriel's mischievous gaze. "No. However, if I plan to get a tree from the Christmas-tree farm, I'll need some lights. I've only had a prelit tree."

"In that case, now would be the time to purchase them before they're picked over."

While he had a point, the motto First Things First came to mind. She made a right toward the paint section, Aggie at her side while Gabriel followed.

An unexpected giddiness came over Jillian as she approached the plethora of paint chips. So many beautiful colors in one place. Each with a personality of its own, calling to mind projects beyond just the walls.

She scrutinized multiple shades of greige while Gabriel explored other colors and, in no time, had a significant stack of chips in her hand.

"Have you decided which room you're going to use for the nursery?" Standing near multiple shades of pink, he glanced her way.

"Oddly enough, no."

"In that case, may I make a recommendation?"

He never ceased to surprise her. "Of course."

"The bedroom with the broken window. It has two walls of windows, so it'll be nice and bright, but that oak in the back will prevent it from being overwhelmingly so."

The man had some great insight. "You make

a good point. Not to mention things will be quieter at the back of the house."

He grinned. "That leads me to my next question. Will you be painting it?" Holding up a pale pink sample, he waggled his eyebrows.

A tall, thin man close to their age with dark hair and eyes approached Gabriel from behind. "I thought I recognized that voice."

Gabriel's smile was instantaneous. He turned to face the man. "Micah!"

The two men shook hands before sharing a manly hug.

"Where have you been keeping yourself?" Gabriel asked when they parted.

"Still teaching here in Brenham." Hands now in the pockets of his faded jeans, the other man shrugged. "Staying at my mom's, helping her out around the farm."

Facing her now, Gabriel said, "Jillian, I'd like you to meet Micah Stallings. We grew up together."

She approached the duo. "It's nice to meet you, Micah." After a brief pause, she added, "Stallings? Are you related to Tori?" Jillian knew her from Sunday school.

"She's my sister-in-law."

"Ah."

As Gabriel continued to pepper his friend with questions, she caught his gaze. "I'm good here—"

she held up the paint chips "—so Aggie and I are going to go explore the Christmas stuff."

"Do you need me...?" he started, but she cut him off.

"I'm perfectly fine. You two take as long as you like." Moving her gaze to the other man, she said, "It was nice to meet you, Micah."

With an air of confidence that had eluded her for far too long, she continued toward the rows of illuminated trees and brightly colored displays. Perhaps she would go ahead and get those lights today.

"What do you think, Aggie? Colored or white?"

The dog looked up at her blankly.

"No opinion, huh?" Hmm, maybe they had lights that could do both, changing with the touch of a button. Though they'd likely be more expensive.

Two little girls rushed past her and Aggie just then.

"You can't catch me," one said with a giggle. Then she darted away as the other girl raced after her.

They had far more energy than she did.

Locating the aisle with the light displays, she studied her options. They did have the lights with the changing colors, but they were priced even higher than she expected, eliminating that option from her list. Back to decision-making.

While she pondered, she continued down the aisle, looking at everything from wreaths to outdoor decorations. She was rounding onto the main aisle near the door to the outdoor lawn and garden center, when the same two girls came racing in her direction once again. Jillian quickly dodged out of their way. Her ballet flat hit something slippery. A gasp escaped her lips, and she let go of Aggie's leash, her arms flailing in a hapless effort to remain upright. Until her feet went out from under her, and down she went.

Her bottom hit the concrete, sending shock waves throughout her body.

She lay there momentarily, trying to regain her wits while Aggie repeatedly nudged her with her wet nose.

"Ma'am! Are you okay?"

She opened her eyes as a female associate knelt beside her. "I—I don't know."

"Did you hit your head?"

"No."

"Jillian!" Gabriel jogged toward her, his friend not far behind him. Kneeling beside her, he said, "What happened?"

"I slipped on something." She groaned as she sat up.

"She says she didn't hit her head," the other woman said.

"That's good," acknowledged Gabriel. "But she's pregnant, so any trauma is a concern."

"Oh, no." The woman stood as an older man approached. A manager, if Jillian was to guess.

"What happened?" He seemed to scrutinize everything and everyone.

"She said she slipped," the woman offered.

"This floor is wet." Gabriel pointed to a small section beside her.

"She's pregnant," the woman told the other man.

"Call 9-1-1," he said. "Tell them to make it fast."

As Jillian's shock began to wear off, mortification set in. "That won't be necessary." When she attempted to stand, Gabriel slipped an arm around her waist and helped her to her feet. And he didn't let go, even once she was upright.

"I'm sorry, miss," the man said. "We'll need to collect information and have you checked out for insurance purposes."

She looked up at Gabriel, noting the mixture of understanding and compassion in his eyes, along with something else. Regret?

"He's right," he said. "Besides, we need to make sure the baby is okay."

Just when she was starting to feel a little more like her old self. Yet while she knew he was right, it pained her knowing that she'd become a burden to him once again.

* * *

The following afternoon, Gabriel bid farewell to his last appointment—a pregnant feline and her overanxious owner—then checked his phone to see if he had any missed calls.

Nothing.

Yet no matter how much he itched to text Jillian or stop by the library to see how she was feeling and how her first day was going, he couldn't do it. After what happened yesterday at the hospital, he needed to take a step back.

He'd always been the calm, levelheaded guy, even in the midst of a crisis. But when he saw Jillian on the floor of the home-improvement center yesterday, looking more than a little dazed, it had taken every ounce of energy he possessed not to come unglued. All he could think about was the child growing inside of her, and how devastated Jillian would be if anything happened to her baby girl.

Thankfully, they were both safe. Jillian said her tailbone was a little sore, but thanks to the sonogram they did at the hospital, they were able to determine the baby was perfectly fine and as active as ever. Still, seeing Jillian's baby in such detail—her little fingers, tiny nose, even sucking her thumb—had done a real number on him, evoking a sense of protectiveness he'd do well to keep in check. He'd already experienced the pain of losing someone he cared about. He didn't care to go through it again.

Continuing to the kennels, he checked on the boxer that had undergone surgery for a fractured leg. Barely awake from the anesthesia, she looked at him with glazed eyes.

He gave her a reassuring rub, wishing he could've talked Doc into gas anesthesia. If he had, Roxie would be feeling much better. "It's all right, girl. Your family will be here soon."

As he walked away, his thoughts again went to Jillian, as they had ever since she'd arrived in Hope Crossing. Only four days and she already consumed his thoughts. Yeah, he needed some distance, all right.

And how are you going to do that when the grandmas want you to work together on the bazaar and *you promised to help Jillian with her house?*

Heaving a sigh, he exited the clinic's side door. While he'd never told anyone, six months ago he'd been contemplating a move to Dallas. He was frustrated with Doc, and a future with Jillian had seemed promising. Then, suddenly, she wanted nothing to do with him.

His pride wasn't the only thing that had taken a hit. His heart took a beating, too. And he never wanted to go through that again.

Determining not to dwell on Jillian, he continued to his vet truck, squinting against the sun. He was slated to be at a local horse farm first thing in the morning for wellness exams, so he wanted to gather everything now so he could head straight there without having to come by the clinic.

In the shade of an oak tree, he went through the various compartments in the truck's bed, mentally noting what was missing, before going back inside. It felt sort of strange not having Aggie with him. He hadn't realized how accustomed he'd gotten to having her around and kind of missed the companionship. But knowing Jillian needed Aggie far more than he did made the loss less painful.

Now that Jillian was working at the library, Gabriel prayed she'd find plenty of good things to occupy her mind. Things that would not only remind her how capable she was but fill her with ideas to breathe new life into the sleepy little library the way she planned to do with Ida Mae's house.

He reached for the door handle, shaking his head. So much for not thinking about Jillian.

In the supply room, he gathered syringes, gloves and testing supplies and ran those to the truck before returning for vaccines and other pharmaceuticals. But after a thorough search for dewormer, he came up empty-handed.

Strange. Doc had put in an order last week. It should've been here long before now.

Exiting the supply room, he sought out the older vet, catching up with him as he exited one of the examination rooms.

"Hey, Doc? Where's that horse dewormer you ordered last week?"

The man peered up at Gabriel, seemingly perplexed. "I didn't order any dewormer. We have plenty."

"No, I told you we were running low." Doc refused to release control and allow Gabriel to place any orders, leaving him at Doc's mercy. "I'm heading over to Rolling Hills tomorrow morning for wellness exams."

"You must be looking in the wrong place." The man shuffled into the supply room and opened the cabinet. After studying the contents for a long moment, he frowned. "I thought for sure..." He sighed. "Well, I reckon you'd best call around and see if you can borrow some from another clinic."

Not an uncommon practice. The borrowing vet simply had a replacement order sent to the clinic that had loaned the meds. But first Gabriel had to locate what he needed, then he'd have to go pick it up. And since they were the only vets in Hope Crossing... Lord willing, he wouldn't have to drive far.

After a few phone calls, Gabriel managed to

come up with an adequate supply for tomorrow. Though, it meant driving to two different clinics in two different towns. Since the one in Brenham was open until six while the one in Bellville closed at five thirty, he'd go to Bellville first.

He double-checked to be sure he had everything else and gave Doc the information for the replacement orders before heading out, making a mental note to check tomorrow and ensure Doc had followed through.

Gabriel turned on his favorite Christian radio station, praying the songs of hope would drown out the turmoil swirling inside of him. Until his phone rang and his mother's name appeared on the dash display.

He tapped the button on his steering wheel. "Hi, Mama."

"How's my baby boy today?"

"Frustrated."

"What's going on?" Concern filled her voice.

"Oh, just something at the clinic. No big deal." Wishing he'd kept his thoughts to himself, he said, "Are you calling to check on Mamaw?" His folks often called him to confirm Mamaw was as fine as she always claimed to be.

"No, I already spoke with her. She was telling me about this Christmas Bazaar she and Ida Mae are spearheading for the youth. She also mentioned that Jillian had moved to Hope Crossing and that you two are going to be overseeing things. *Together.*"

Continuing down the farm-to-market road, he eyed rolling hills dotted with cattle. "Yes. Jillian is Hope Crossing's new library director."

"How do you feel about that? I mean, the two of you had been spending quite a lot of time together earlier this year. And while I have no idea what happened to change that, I know you weren't happy about it."

"How do you know that?"

"Because I'm your mother. You might think you can hide things from me, but I can tell when something's not right with my children."

No arguing that. Yet while her mama-bear tendencies bugged him at times, he knew they were born of love. Still, he wasn't about to break Jillian's confidence by going into her story with his mother. Not without her permission. He would, however, have to throw his mother a bone.

"Jillian and I are getting along just fine. Remember Aggie?"

"The dog you inherited?"

"That's correct. She's now Jillian's dog."

"But I thought you liked Aggie."

He chuckled at the pout in her tone. "I do. But I didn't *need* her. Aggie is a trained service dog. She needs to be needed."

There was a long pause. "Are you saying Jillian needs her?"

"That's exactly what I'm saying." Maneuvering a sharp curve, he added, "Look, I'm not at liberty to share. Just know that when it comes to Jillian and me, there were some extenuating circumstances. She's struggling. So if you're inclined to do so, she could use your prayers."

"I'm sorry to hear that. She's always been so sweet. I'm glad you're able to be there for her and am adding her to my prayer list right now."

"Thank you. So what's going on with you and Dad?" He listened while she went on about his father's golf game, her garden club and their two grandchildren. His sister Annie's kiddos had been a driving force behind Dad accepting a job in Georgetown five years ago. And Gabriel was fairly certain his folks would remain there once Dad retired next year.

Approaching Bellville, he reduced his speed. "Mama, I need to let you go. I'm almost at my stop, and I'm kind of in a hurry."

"All right, hon. We'll chat later."

Gravel ground beneath his tires as Gabriel entered the clinic's parking lot. Thankfully, they had what he needed waiting at the front desk, affording him a quick turnaround.

Back behind the wheel, he continued on to Brenham, thoughts of Jillian and the tiny life growing inside her wreaking havoc on his brain. While she knew a few people in Hope Crossing, he was her friend. They'd gotten to know each other quite well these past couple of years. If only they had remained friends. That would've made the situation now much easier.

But that hadn't happened. Instead, friendship had blossomed into something more. Something unexpected and wonderful. Something he'd never found with any other woman. Something that had had him contemplating leaving Hope Crossing.

Did that mean they weren't friends, though?

I'm glad you're able to be there for her. His mother's words replayed in his mind.

Was he willing to leave Jillian floundering because things hadn't turned out the way he'd hoped?

A friend loveth at all times, and a brother is born for adversity.

The verse from Proverbs played across his mind.

Gabriel shook his head as he maneuvered around a slow-moving tractor. "Okay, God, I get it. Jillian and I are still friends." He paused for a moment, pondering the second half of the verse. Friends were imperative when times were tough, which was why he'd always tried to be a good one. Friends prayed for one another, comforted them, were there for them.

He tapped his brakes as the speed limit dropped. His desire for distance had been born of selfishness. His own unease and loss, not Jillian's. Which paled in comparison to what she had endured and was still enduring.

He needed to get over himself and be the friend he claimed to be.

His phone rang again, and Jillian's name appeared on the screen.

"Hey, there. How was your first day on the job?"

"Very enjoyable." Though there was a smile in her voice, she sounded tired. "I think I'm really going to like this new position."

"Good."

"Do you have dinner plans?"

He eyed a couple of fast-food places as he rolled into Brenham. "Nothing solid. Why?"

"Because I'd like to invite you for dinner. My way of saying thank you for everything you've done for me lately. I know I haven't been the easiest neighbor."

"You haven't heard me complain, have you?" Approaching his turn, he switched on his blinker.

"No, which is why it's time I did something nice for you. I put a pot roast in the slow cooker this morning."

"Your house must smell amazing."

"Oh, yes. Aggie's been walking around with her nose in the air ever since we got home."

He'd seen the poodle do that before.

"I still have to bake the rolls, but they won't take long. So what do you say?"

He made another turn. "I'm in Brenham right now."

"Oh."

The disappointment in her tone had him forging ahead. "But I just have to pick up something from one of the vet clinics here, then I'll be on my way home. I can be there in, say, thirty, forty-five minutes?"

"Sounds great. I'll see you then."

He ended the call, his gaze drifting to the puffy clouds floating aimlessly overhead. "I get it, God. I need to be the friend You've called me to be. Just, please, help me to keep my heart in check this time."

Chapter Five

While Jillian wasn't sure what normal was anymore, by Wednesday she was feeling pretty good. Her anxiety had diminished, despite publicly embarrassing herself at the home-improvement center Sunday. Poor Gabriel. When he'd insisted they go look at paint colors, he probably never imagined the journey would end up taking several hours. Thankfully, her pride and tailbone were the only things that had suffered from that ridiculous fall.

In addition to Aggie's help, getting back to work, doing what she loved yet being forced to look at it from a different angle, had occupied Jillian's mind enough that it had kept all those unwanted thoughts at bay. And for that, she was grateful.

"Have you met Alli Walker?" Standing atop a colorful rug in the middle of the small library's children's section late Wednesday afternoon, Rita continued walking Jillian through the various events the library hosted.

"Yes, at the football game Friday." Aggie at her side, Jillian eyed the woman she'd be replacing. "She mentioned the Children's Story Hour and the possibility of expanding it."

"Oh, good. She spoke with me, as well, but I thought it would be best to hold off until you took over. I will say, it's an event the children look forward to all month. It's very well attended."

"Really?" Jillian would've thought a weekday would be better attended. But then, by having it on Saturdays, early elementary children were also able to attend. And given that the population of Hope Crossing was so small to begin with, she supposed Saturdays did make more sense.

"Ever since Alli took over the readings this past spring, participation has grown considerably. But I shouldn't be surprised. Alli's engaging reading style was what had me asking her to join us in the first place."

"I'm excited to hear her, then. I'm a firm believer in instilling a love for the written word from an early age."

"Hear! Hear!" Rita's gaze moved from Jillian's face to her abdomen and back. "How are you feeling, dear?"

"So far, so good." Awkwardness had her

reaching for Aggie. In situations like this, she always felt as though she was hiding a secret. Which she supposed she was. With most women, it could be assumed the child's father was the woman's husband or at least someone she actually knew and had some sort of relationship with. But Jillian knew zero about her baby's father. And while she wasn't ashamed of her baby, the circumstances surrounding it weren't the kind of thing one brought up in general conversation.

"I assume the learning center will be able to accommodate your little one once he or she arrives?" Rita's matter-of-fact tone helped put her at ease.

"Yes." Jillian's other hand moved to her belly. "The doctor says it's a little girl."

The graying brunette beamed. "Oh, how precious."

An electronic bell dinged and had them both turning toward the entrance as a petite blonde entered with a little boy who looked to be around four.

"All right, Aiden." The woman glanced at her watch. "You've got thirty minutes before they close. Then we've got church."

"'Kay." The dark-haired boy started toward Jillian and Rita, coming up short when he spotted Aggie. "Whoa… I didn't know they allowed dogs in the library."

His mother, Tori, who Jillian knew from Sunday school, moved beside him. "Only certain dogs." She looked from Aggie to her son. "Aggie is a service dog."

The boy's face scrunched as he peered up at his mother. "What's a serbice dog?"

"Ser*vice* dogs are specially trained to help people with lots of things. They can help those who can't see or hear or who have a medical condition like high blood pressure."

The boy looked from his mom to Aggie and then to Jillian. "What does your dog help you with?"

"Oh." Jillian froze. What should she say? That she was afraid of everything? A scaredy-cat, as kids would say. "I—"

"Aiden, that's none of our business. All you need to know is that Aggie is working. That means you can't play with her like you would a regular dog."

"Oh." His gaze darted between Jillian and the dog. "Aggie must get bored. Dogs like to play."

"Yes, they do," offered Jillian. "So when I take off Aggie's vest, she knows she's not working anymore and is able to play."

The boy stared at Aggie, seemingly trying to absorb all of the information. "Mama, do you think they have any books about ser*vice* dogs?"

"They might." Tori glanced at Rita.

"Come on, Aiden." Rita motioned for the boy to follow her. "Let's have a look on this shelf over here." She led him to a series of shelves at his eye level.

"Sorry about that." Tori watched after her son.

Jillian waved off the comment. "There's nothing to be sorry about. Kids learn by asking questions." Turning an eye to the boy, she added, "The fact that he's looking for a book about service dogs says his interest was piqued."

"Curiosity is his middle name."

Jillian returned her attention to Tori. "Did I hear you say you were going to church tonight?"

"Yes. It's a challenge to get there sometimes, being a single mom, but tonight's the first rehearsal for the children's Christmas pageant, and Aiden has his heart set on being a donkey."

They both chuckled.

"We all have aspirations," said Jillian.

"Are you coming for Bible study?"

"I didn't know there was one, but that's something I would like to be a part of. Tonight I'm attending the Christmas Bazaar meeting."

"I heard about that. Wait." Tori's blue eyes brightened. "It's your grandmother organizing it along with Ms. Milly."

"Yes. However, they've appointed me and Gabriel as their *representatives.*" Jillian punctuated that last word with air quotes.

Tori chuckled. "Knowing Ms. Ida Mae and Ms. Milly, that doesn't surprise me. Those two are a couple of go-getters."

"You have no idea." Jillian thought back to the first day she'd arrived at the assisted living. The way Grandmama just expected Jillian and Gabriel to work together, as if the last several months had never happened.

"Well, I think it's a fantastic idea. If they get some good donations and a lot of promotion, it could play out really well." Tori touched a finger to her chin. "I wonder if Gloriana is planning to help with promotion. That's kind of her thing." She looked at Jillian. "Have you met Gloriana?"

"The name sounds familiar. Was she in Gabriel's Sunday-school class?"

"Yes, until she married Justin Broussard last fall. Her daughter is in the youth group, though, so I imagine she'd be happy to help get the word out."

Aiden scurried toward them, his smile wide. "Mama, I found one."

"Good deal, little man. Let's find you a couple more, and then we've got to go."

Once Tori and her son departed, Jillian and Rita locked the doors and went their separate ways. Jillian had just enough time to grab a quick bite to eat and allow Aggie to run around the yard some before Jillian and Gabriel had to leave to pick up the grandmas.

Gabriel was getting out of his truck when she pulled into the drive a few minutes later. What was it about the sight of him that always made her smile?

He waited for her to emerge from her car. "How was your day?" He petted Aggie, who'd raced to his side.

"Good." She closed her door. "Rita is very thorough and runs a tight ship, so I think the transition is going very well."

"Glad to hear it." He seemed hesitant.

"Is something wrong?"

"Not really. The guy from the glass company just called. He's on his way out to take a look at your window, which means I need to be here to meet him. I should still be able to make it to the meeting. However, I might be a little late. Would you mind picking up the grandmas, and I'll join you just as soon as possible?"

He shouldn't have to ask. Not after everything he'd done for her. "Of course not. Are you sure you don't want me to stay, though? It is my window, after all."

"That's up to you." Hands in the pockets of his jeans, he shrugged. "I just assumed—I mean, I don't want you to feel uncomfortable."

Her cheeks grew warm. "Thank you. You're right. And no, I don't mind getting the grandmas."

He smiled. "Good. I shouldn't be too far behind you."

"Do you think I should leave Aggie here?"

He shook his head. "You're still getting used to each other, so that's not a good idea."

"But what if there's an issue with one of the grandmas?"

"Then, you'll have Aggie there to help."

"Good point." Lifting a brow, she said, "Care to join me for a sandwich?" She probably shouldn't have asked. After all, they'd been thrown together enough this past week. He might welcome a reprieve.

He rocked back on his heels. "Best offer I've had all day."

When she left thirty minutes later to pick up the grandmas, Jillian couldn't help thinking she was starting to feel a little more at ease in her new life here in Hope Crossing and prayed it would continue.

After collecting Grandmama and Ms. Milly, Jillian continued to the church. She rolled to a stop at the entrance to the youth barn, then exited to retrieve the two walkers that barely fit into her trunk and assisted the older women emerging from the front and back seats.

As they started toward the entrance, Jillian said, "I'll join you in a minute."

The parking lot between the youth barn and

the steepled beige brick building that was the church was at least half-full. Pretty substantial for a Wednesday evening, at least compared to her previous church in Dallas.

She exited her car, locking it before clipping the leash to Aggie's collar. "Let's go find the grandmas, girl."

When she pulled open the glass door of the beige metal building, a popular contemporary Christian song spilled from inside. Stepping onto the gray carpet, she saw a couple of women to her left, chatting behind a check-in desk that had been made from pallet wood, while a trio of boys clustered near a cozy gathering space to her right with a sofa and love seat separated by a coffee table. Meanwhile, more voices and laughter drifted from a larger gymnasium-style space beyond the open double doors on the wall in front of her.

Not seeing either of the grandmas, Jillian assumed they'd gone on into the big room.

Just then, a woman close to Jillian's age, perhaps a little older, approached. "May I help you?"

"I'm here for the Christmas Bazaar meeting."

The brunette tilted her head. "I don't believe we've met. Are you a member here?"

"It's okay, Tracy. She's with me."

Jillian turned as Gabriel approached.

"Oh." The woman looked from Gabriel to Jillian's stomach, then back to Gabriel. "I wasn't aware."

"Jillian, this is Tracy Hubbard. Tracy, this is Jillian McKenna, Ms. Ida Mae's granddaughter."

"I see." Again, Tracy's brow lifted, her gaze continuing to bounce between Gabriel and Jillian's baby bump. "It's nice to meet you."

"Likewise."

Touching Jillian's elbow, Gabriel steered her away from Tracy, smiling at a couple of teenage girls as though everything was just fine. "How are you ladies tonight?"

"Good," they said in unison, though one punctuated hers with a titter.

Yet while Gabriel might be at ease, continuing to greet people as he guided her into the large room with rows of chairs slowly filling with youth and adults alike, Jillian suddenly became horrifyingly aware that her condition might be putting Gabriel in a compromising situation. After all, up until her attack, they had been very close. Even holding hands in church occasionally. What if someone suspected Gabriel was her baby's father?

Something wasn't right.

Ever since the meeting at church Wednesday night, Jillian had been avoiding him. Her house was dark when he came home from dropping off the grandmas that night and when he'd left the next morning. Her text messages had been rather cryptic, too. Like back in May when she'd stopped communicating with him.

And while that had alarm bells going off in his head, this was different. He knew it beyond a shadow of a doubt. He just couldn't put his finger on the problem.

Now as he pulled into the parking lot at the senior living just after twelve thirty Saturday afternoon, he eyed Jillian's car. Suspecting she'd stop by to visit Ms. Ida Mae after the library closed at noon, he'd been purposeful in his timing. He just hoped it would pay off. After all, they were supposed to pick up a couple of donations near Round Top today. Though, with the way things had been going, he wouldn't be surprised if Jillian tried to find a way out of her commitment.

After parking, he continued into the building. Noting that only a few stragglers remained in the dining room, he went on to Mamaw's room. He knocked, then opened the door a crack and called her name. When he got no response, he went next door to Ms. Ida Mae's room.

Approaching the door that had been left cracked open, he could hear the conversation taking place inside.

"It's not me I'm worried about, it's Gabriel."

Why was Jillian worried about him?

Only one way to find out.

He rapped his knuckles against the door. "Mamaw? You in there?"

"Come on in, Gabriel."

At the sound of Ms. Ida Mae's voice, he eased the door open and stepped inside, where he found the two older women seated while Jillian remained standing, looking as though she'd been caught divulging state secrets. Her cheeks grew pinker by the second while her gaze darted between the grandmas, as though pleading for help. What was that all about?

Addressing Mamaw, he said, "When you weren't in your room, I figured I'd find you here."

"Jillian was just sharing some concerns with us," Ida Mae offered.

He looked at a seemingly horrified Jillian. "What sort of concerns?"

"Oh." She waved one hand while the other nervously rubbed Aggie. "It was noth—"

"Before you continue, you should know that I heard my name mentioned. Why are you worried about me, Jillian?" Whatever it was might explain why she'd been avoiding him, too.

All eyes were on her as she, seemingly, struggled with whatever it was that had her concerned.

Finally, with a hefty sigh, she said, "At the meeting Wednesday night. That woman. Tracy."

"What about her?"

"Did you see the look on her face when you said I was with you?"

"No."

Jillian's eyes widened, her brows lifting. "As soon as you announced I was with you, she looked as though she was watching a tennis match, the way her judgmental gaze darted back and forth between my stomach and your face."

"I guess I was so focused on getting to our meeting that I missed that, but so what? Why does that have you worried about me?"

Shaking her head, she looked at her grandmother. "Why do men have to be so clueless?"

"Like I said, Jilly—" her grandmother wagged a crooked finger "—I wouldn't worry one iota what folks like that think. They're just trying to stir up trouble."

His frustration growing, Gabriel said, "Would somebody please explain to me what Jillian is so worried about?"

Wearing a frown that was somewhere between annoyed and sorrowful, she said, "Because you have a reputation to uphold. If it were to become tarnished because of me, I'd never forgive myself."

Suddenly it all made sense. "Is that why you've been avoiding me?"

Arms wound around herself, she nodded.

He couldn't help but grin. "Jillian, are you trying to defend my honor?"

“This isn’t funny, Gabriel. You are a respected member of this community, while I’m a pregnant stranger.”

Mamaw scowled and reached for Jillian’s hand. “Child, you have *nothing* to be ashamed of, you hear me? Forget about those gossipmongers. They’d like nothing more than to tear you down, but don’t give them the satisfaction of fretting over their opinions. It’s not good for you or your baby.”

Gabriel couldn’t remember the last time he’d seen his grandmother so emphatic. Yet he understood why. She and Jillian had far more in common than Jillian knew.

He looked at Jillian. “She’s right, you know.”

Jillian’s shoulders dropped a notch. “It’s still infuriating.”

“Jilly, you’re just borrowing trouble, and you’d best stop it right now,” Ida Mae scolded. “You need to find something else to occupy your mind.”

“And I have just the thing.” Gabriel looked around to find three curious pairs of eyes watching him. “What? We’ve got donations to pick up.” Turning his attention to Jillian, he added, “And that living room of yours isn’t going to paint itself.” Once Jillian had decided earlier this week which shade of greige she preferred, he’d gone ahead and picked up the paint and supplies.

Looking suddenly sheepish, she said, "I forgot we were going to do that."

"Yeah, well, now that I've reminded you, it's time to hop to it. Besides, the Aggies are playing later, and I don't want to miss the kickoff."

"Can I at least eat lunch first?" She draped her purse over one shoulder and took Aggie's leash in her other hand.

"I'll allow you a sandwich for the road."

After a round of hugs, they started for the door.

"No ladders for you, young lady," her grandmother warned.

Gabriel reached for the handle. "Don't worry, Ms. Ida Mae. I'll keep her grounded."

Exiting the building minutes later, he said, "Your grandmother's right." He touched Jillian's elbow, stopping on the sidewalk, midway between the building and the parking lot. "You don't know what Tracy was thinking. You're purely speculating."

Her blue eyes met his as the breeze tossed her auburn tresses across her face. Did he dare tuck them behind her ear the way he used to? Revel in their softness?

She beat him to it. "Don't you see? I used to think that way. Playing judge and jury, deeming people guilty without knowing the facts." She lowered her head. "Now I'm getting a taste of my own medicine."

"I think most of us are guilty of that at one time or another. But you're not doing yourself or your baby any favors. So please, just try to forget the whole thing. Okay?" When all she did was shrug, he added, "Otherwise I might have to tickle you." One of things he'd learned about her in their all-too-brief time as a quasicouple was that Jillian was so ticklish she could even tickle herself.

Her eyes narrowed. "You wouldn't."

Straightening, he crossed his arms over his chest. "Care to try me?"

She watched him for a long moment. "Sometimes you can be such a brat." Her eyes sparkled as she playfully shoved him.

"Come on." He nodded toward their vehicles. "We have some donations to pick up."

"And don't forget the painting," she added. "I cannot wait to bid those peachy walls adieu."

Stuffing his hands in the pockets of his tattered jeans, he smiled as he turned for his truck. That little bit of playfulness just now had given him a glimpse of the old Jillian. The one who'd been carefree, bold and full of life. He could only hope to see more of her as the day went on.

Feeling a hand on his elbow, he stopped.

Jillian looked suddenly shy as she peered up at him. "Thank you, Gabriel, for all you've done. You're a good friend."

Friend. While he always tried to put others first and was quick to lend a helping hand, when it came to women, *friend* tended to be a dirty little word. It meant the likelihood of him being anything more than that was slim to none. Until Jillian came along.

Yet while he knew she needed his friendship and he wanted to be there for her, he couldn't forget the way things used to be. The anticipation of seeing each other, trying to squeeze the most out of the times they were together, the video chats that would last late into the night because neither wanted to say goodbye.

He'd like to throttle the jerk who'd stolen so much from her. But if *friend* was the label he had to wear to be a part of Jillian's life, he'd continue to wear it proudly. Even if it felt like a scratchy sweater.

Chapter Six

"What do you mean Dad and Marshall are on their way?" Jillian turned away from the circulation desk shortly after ten the following Saturday, phone pressed to her ear as she started toward her office with Aggie beside her.

"Ethan's ball game was canceled after the other team had to forfeit." Ethan was Jillian's nephew. "Seems a party last night left several of the players with food poisoning," her mother continued. "And you know neither your father nor your brother likes to be idle, so they picked up a trailer this morning and went to your storage unit to start loading."

"They're not bringing everything, are they?"

"Knowing the two of them, I would not be surprised."

But Grandmama's house was already full of furniture. Where would Jillian put everything?

She eyed her watch. “Have they left yet?” She could call and talk them through what to bring and what to leave.

“About thirty minutes ago.”

She slumped against the doorway of her office. That would put their arrival time around one thirty or two, depending on traffic. Considering she didn’t get off work until noon, that didn’t allow her much time to prepare. Not only was there no room for her furniture while Grandmama’s things were still in place, she’d also need to make up the beds in the other two bedrooms. Surely they wouldn’t turn right around and drive home tonight. Not that she’d put it past them. Still, she preferred to be ready, just in case. At least the window in the back bedroom had finally been replaced.

Then she remembered the plans she and Gabriel had made for today. After picking up a few more donations this afternoon, they were driving to Houston for some shopping and dinner. She’d been craving Mexican food, so he’d mentioned his favorite restaurant. One they’d gone to together earlier this year.

“Oh, no!”

“What is it, dear?”

“I already have plans with—” She almost said *Gabriel*. “With a friend.” Jillian didn’t want her mother reading too much into their relationship.

"You'll just have to postpone them."

Easy for her to say. Jillian, on the other hand, had been looking forward to them all week. Had even awakened this morning, feeling like a schoolgirl brimming with anticipation.

"I need to go, Mom. Thank you for the heads-up. I appreciate it." Ending the call, Jillian tucked her phone into the back pocket of her jeans, shaking her head.

"Problem?"

She snapped her head up at the sound of Gabriel's voice. "When did you…?"

"While you were on the phone. You were lost in conversation, so I didn't want to bother you." Despite this morning's cool temperatures, he wore his usual gameday attire—jeans and an A&M T-shirt, this one gray with maroon lettering. He strolled closer, his gaze narrowing. "Though, you sounded a little perturbed. Is there a problem?"

Her hand falling to Aggie, Jillian let go a frustrated sigh. "That was my mother. Seems my father and brother are on their way down here with all of my furniture."

"On their…?" He shifted from one booted foot to the other. "Like, now?"

She nodded. "Like they'll probably be here by two."

Hands on his hips, he stared at her. "So we're not going to Houston."

"No. I'm sorry." She burrowed her fists in the pockets of her lightweight gray cardigan.

"Don't apologize. You didn't know."

"But our plans—"

"Can be postponed until next Saturday. Assuming you're available."

Still dealing with her own disappointment, she rocked back on the heels of her ballet flats. "Thank you for understanding."

Staring across the rows of bookshelves, he rubbed his scruffy chin. "I guess we need to figure out what to do with Ida Mae's furniture, huh?"

"I don't have the slightest."

"Let me make a few phone calls. Perhaps there's someone in need who'd like to have some of it." He hesitated. "Though, I guess we oughta check with your grandmother first."

"No, she and I have already discussed it. She said to burn it."

He chuckled. "Probably not the best option."

"I'm sorry, Gabriel." Jillian didn't even try to hide her whine. Though, she managed to refrain from stomping her foot. "I was really looking forward to today."

"Hey, look on the bright side. With your dad, brother and me all working, things'll get done that much quicker. By the time they leave, your place will be almost complete." He shrugged.

"It also means I'll be able to watch the Aggies game."

While she was thrilled he was willing to help… "Uh-oh." She worried her bottom lip.

"What?"

"Dad and Marshall both went to UT." She held up her index and pinkie fingers. "Hook 'em horns."

Slapping a hand against his chest, he stumbled backward in mock horror. "The lady speaketh evil."

She couldn't help laughing. "For what it's worth, I went to a private Christian college in Dallas."

"All right, you get a pass." He rubbed his hands together. "So what can I do for you? Do you need me to pick up some groceries or anything?"

"Good question." She tried to remember what was in her freezer. "Maybe some kolaches from Plowman's for breakfast tomorrow. I know they both like those."

Gabriel puffed out a laugh. "Who doesn't?"

"You have a grill, right?"

"I do."

"I've got some ground beef in the freezer." She clasped her hands together. "I could make hamburgers."

"Do you have any buns?"

"No."

"Have you got anything to go with the burgers? Beans? Chips?"

She slowly shook her head. "Things have been so hectic since I got here that I haven't had time to plan for guests."

"Tell you what." He held up his hands. "Why don't you leave the food to me?"

"Gabriel, I can't let you do that. I mean, I'm sure you have things you'd like to do."

"The only plans I had for today were to do pickups and go to Houston. Now that I'm not doing that..." He shrugged.

"What about the pickups, though? How are we going to fit them in?"

"Easy. I'll take care of them now."

"But the grandmas said we're supposed to do them together."

He winked. "What they don't know won't hurt them."

Crossing her arms over her chest, she sighed. "Will I ever stop finding myself indebted to you?" At least she was able to be a sounding board for him when he'd needed to vent his frustration with Doc. Though, she couldn't help feeling bad for the elderly doctor who, obviously, wasn't ready to stop feeling useful. Still, she hated that it was at Gabriel's expense. The depth of his loyalty was a rare commodity in today's world, and she admired him for it. If only Doc would recognize that.

"Indebted? Hardly. We're friends. That's what friends do. They help each other."

Gabriel was the best friend anyone could ask for. Yet, at one time, their relationship had grown into something more. Now, here they were, back to just friends. Something she supposed she'd have to be satisfied with, because she had too much baggage to even dare hope for anything more.

"Thank you, Gabriel."

"No problem." He started for the door. "I'll see you back at the house."

Jillian spent the next two hours at the library trying to determine what to do about her sudden surplus of furniture. She supposed she'd have to cram as much as possible into the other two bedrooms. On the flip side, she was looking forward to having her bed again. Grandmama's mattress was way too firm.

When she finally pulled up to her house just before twelve thirty, Gabriel was coming out of the small single-car detached garage at his place, wiping his hands on a rag, a satisfied smile on his face.

"What do you suppose he's up to, Aggie girl?"

Perched in the passenger seat, the pooch stared out the window, her tongue hanging.

Gathering her tote, Jillian opened the door and exited, then waited for Aggie to follow. Jillian removed the dog's vest. "Go get him, girl."

Shielding her eyes from the sun, Jillian watched the canine trot across the grass, savoring the near-perfect fall day. Yesterday's front had brought them some blessedly cooler air. Though, right now she was pushing up the sleeves of her sweater and could hardly wait to throw open the windows in her house.

Moving at a more leisurely pace, Jillian approached Gabriel. "What are you working on?"

"Clearing one side of my garage—which pretty much serves as a catchall anyway since neither of my trucks will fit—in case you need space to store some stuff."

Her vision blurred as tears filled her eyes, spilling onto her cheeks. She quickly turned around, not wanting him to see her. But it was too late.

"Hey, what's going on?" He was in front of her, his palms cupping her elbows.

"Nothing," she sobbed, feeling absolutely mortified. "Just stupid pregnancy hormones making me melt down over a random act of kindness." She swiped at her cheeks. "Ugh. This is so embarrassing." She sniffed, finally meeting his gaze. "Thank you. That was very sweet of you. Not to mention unexpected."

"Well, with you getting bigger every day, you'll need space to move around the house."

"Wait. Did you just say I was big?"

His expression was priceless. "Uh, no. I probably should've phrased that differently. The *baby* is getting bigger every day. And you're smiling again."

"I am." A chuckle bubbled from her. "Thanks. Now I need to change clothes and see about making some space in the house."

"Oh, no you don't." He picked up the ball Aggie had dropped at his feet. "You can formulate a plan, but I'm in charge of execution. No heavy lifting for you."

"Yes, sir."

He tossed the ball as she started toward the house. "I'll stay out here and entertain the Aggster for a while. Don't forget to take the ground beef out of the freezer. Rest of the stuff's at my place." He poked a thumb over his shoulder as Aggie trotted toward him with a ball in her mouth. "May as well leave it there until we need it."

Pausing on the porch, she glanced back at Gabriel. How many times had she dreamed of him since her assault? Of being held in his strong arms again and him feeling the same way about her as he once had. Picking up where they left off, only with her living in Hope Crossing.

But that was nothing more than a pipe dream.

Everything he'd done for her since she'd arrived—going out of his way to make her feel safe, helping her out around the house—that was Gabriel's modus operandi. When he saw a need, he went to any length to meet it. Meaning she couldn't allow herself to read anything more into his actions. No matter how much she might want to.

Gabriel hadn't planned to be at the clinic the following Saturday, but Doc had called him around six thirty that morning after receiving an emergency call that someone's dog had been struck by a car. Yet while Doc had been the on-call vet, he'd asked Gabriel to meet the family at the clinic because he wasn't feeling up to it, further fueling Gabriel's suspicion that Doc was slipping.

So after splinting the dog's leg and sending the family on their way, Gabriel decided to take the rest of the morning to inventory the pharmacy. With Doc making more than one error of late, Gabriel didn't want to risk being blindsided again. Besides, it would give him something to do until Jillian got off work at noon.

He took another swig of coffee from his travel mug, surprised at how much he was actually looking forward to this trip to Houston with Jillian. Not that he was all that interested in shopping, even if it was to purchase items for the bazaar. No, it was the thought of spending hours with his beautiful neighbor that had him filled with anticipation. Which was really kind of silly. After all, they were just friends. Not that that had kept him from hanging out at her place just about every night, helping her unpack boxes and arrange furniture.

With the aid of her dad and brother, they'd moved the furniture Jillian didn't want—which was almost everything in the living room, plus the kitchen table and chairs, and a few items from the bedrooms—into his garage well before dinner last Saturday. Then they'd removed the carpet from the living and dining rooms before bringing in Jillian's stuff. Matter of fact, they'd worked so efficiently that the other two men left first thing the next morning, allowing Jillian to accompany Gabriel to church.

Setting his cup aside now, he returned to the task at hand, comparing the actual inventory against orders and prescriptions. Until a noise had him stepping into the hallway shortly after ten thirty.

Doc looked up with a smile as he closed the door behind him. "Gabriel. Didn't expect to see you here."

Gabriel could say the same thing. "I'm going

over things in the pharmacy. Making sure we have adequate inventory."

The older man frowned. "I expect that's a good idea since we've had some problems recently. How are things looking?"

"Pretty good. Though, we seem to have an overabundance of the Clavamox blister packs." While the antibiotic was a common prescription, they never ordered it in such large quantities.

Doc's bushy eyebrows drew together as he rubbed the stubble on his chin. "I wonder why. Do you s'pose they sent us too much?"

"It doesn't appear so." He motioned the man into the supply room. Pausing beside the counter, Gabriel pointed to the packing slip. "Shows here it was ordered on Tuesday."

"I wouldn't order all that." He frowned at Gabriel. "You sure you didn't order it?"

Unwilling to point out that Doc didn't allow him to do any ordering, he said, "I was out of the clinic Tuesday."

The older man's countenance fell. "Oh, that's right." Turning, he shuffled to the opposite side of the space and paused beside the sterilizer, looking somewhat defeated.

Only then did Gabriel recall their phone conversation earlier and the man's uncharacteristic claim that he wasn't feeling well. "You okay, Doc?"

His gaze met Gabriel's. "'Course. I'm thinking, though—" he ran a hand over his thinning white hair "—perhaps it's time you take over the ordering. You understand that computer stuff far better than I ever will."

Gabriel suspected the excess was the result of the man typing in the wrong amount. Like adding an extra zero.

"You wouldn't mind doing that, would you, Gabriel?"

"No." He shook his head. "I don't mind at all." Despite Doc adding more to Gabriel's plate all the time.

"Good. Good." The man nodded as he shuffled out of the room. "'Preciate you, son."

"Doc?"

The man turned.

"What brings you in today?"

"Need to check on a patient."

"What patient?" The kennels were empty.

"The Millers' dog."

"They picked him up last night, Doc."

"They did?" The man's faded blue eyes widened.

"Right before closing."

The man rubbed his chin. "Guess I missed that." He chuckled. "In that case, I'm goin' back home. Got some chores waitin' on me." Perhaps he was feeling better.

Yet as Gabriel watched the man exit the building, he couldn't help noticing just how quickly Doc's age seemed to be catching up to him. Especially since Ms. Lavonne's passing last year. And that had Gabriel concerned about his future at the clinic.

Lord, please give Doc the clarity to realize it's time for him to step down and turn things over to me like he promised.

Maybe Gabriel would suggest Doc cut down on the number of hours he spent at the clinic. It would be a start anyway, to kind of ease him into retirement.

With his mission completed five minutes before noon, Gabriel locked up and headed home, only to have Jillian pull into the drive next to his as he got out of his truck. He couldn't help smiling when he saw her and was glad they were able to squeeze in their trip today. Since it was only the first weekend in November, things should still be about the same as any other Saturday. All too soon, though, the crowds would build to that holiday hustle and bustle he did his best to avoid.

"I just need to freshen up and then we can go." Under a sunny sky, Jillian closed her car door once Aggie hopped out.

"No rush. I'll try to wear Aggie out with the ball."

The dog bounded toward him, and he removed

her vest. "You ready for a little play time?" Aggie had made a real difference in Jillian. Though Jillian still struggled on occasion, Aggie was always right there to offer comfort and strength. They were almost inseparable. Which had him thinking. Perhaps Aggie would appreciate a little downtime.

So when Jillian again joined them, he said, "What would you think about giving Aggie some time off? That is, if you'd be comfortable without her. Then again, with stores being busier on the weekends…" He shrugged. "It's your call. I just thought I'd throw it out there."

"Actually, I've been wondering if I'm overworking her. I mean, she's always on call, so to speak."

"I don't know that she's overworked, but just like us, they enjoy some me time every now and then. I just don't want you doing anything that'll make you uneasy."

Her blue eyes lifted to his. "You'll be with me, right?"

Something in the way she looked at him had him standing a little taller. "You can count on it, Jillian."

"In that case, let's give Aggie the day off."

They hit the road shortly after one and filled the almost-hour-long trip talking about the grandmas and what transpired at the clinic this morning.

After lunch at a popular Mexican grill, they continued on to Jillian's favorite superstore. Since she had sorted through her things before moving, and he leaned more toward minimalism, they'd opted to purchase their donations for the bazaar. And it wasn't long before the red shopping cart was brimming with preschool toys, dolls, a couple of remote-control monster trucks and more.

Strolling the aisles of Christmas decorations, Jillian began to grin. "Do you hear that?" She pointed toward the ceiling.

He listened. "Seriously? We're barely into November and they're playing Christmas music."

"Well, I like it." She gave him a playful shove. "Stop being such a Scrooge."

After adding a couple more items to the cart, they continued along one of the main aisles.

When Jillian's steps slowed, Gabriel noticed her gaze drifting to their left. He followed her line of sight, realizing it was the baby section that had caught her eye.

He aimed the cart in that direction. "Let's go have a look."

"No, we don't—"

"Jillian, how many things have you bought for your baby?" Because aside from choosing a paint color for the nursery, he hadn't seen or heard her mention anything. Quite a contrast to his sister, who began collecting things almost from the moment she found out she was pregnant.

"I've done some perusing online. I just haven't purchased anything yet."

"You know your baby will be here in only a few short months, right?"

"No, that completely slipped my mind." The corners of her mouth lifted as she shook her head. "Of course I'm aware."

"And you may as well deduct at least two weeks off that for the holidays. Which will also leave everything picked over, so your selection will be limited."

"All right." She huffed. "We can look."

Following her, he said, "You should at least get a few basics. Sleepers, blankets, bottles, *diapers*."

She whisked past a rack of miniature flannel shirts. "How do you know so much about what babies need?"

"My sister. Before kids, Annie felt the need to include me in almost every aspect of her life. So when she was pregnant with her first, she was determined to have me walk that road with her. She'd video call me from stores to get my input."

"That is so sweet."

Not nearly as sweet as Jillian's smile.

"I wish my siblings would've included me more." She paused beside a row of strollers. "Alexandra was busy trying to craft the perfect life for herself and her family, and Marshall was laser-focused on his career."

"And what were you doing?"

"Rising in the ranks at the Dallas library. Fixing up my house." She scrunched her cute nose. "Sounds kind of boring, doesn't it?"

"No. It sounds like my life. You won't have to worry about *boring* much longer, though, because your baby is going to shake things up."

Her hand went to her rounded tummy. "As if she hasn't already." Lifting her eyes, she craned her neck before moving to the next aisle.

He followed her. "What do you see?"

"That." Stopping, she pointed to a pretty white crib with an arched side.

"Nice." He glanced her way. "Do you like it?"

"I do. It's modern, but still classic in design."

Returning his attention to the crib, he said, "You're right about that." He again met her gaze. "Why don't you get it?"

She worried her bottom lip, still pondering the crib. "I don't know."

"Would you prefer to look at some others?"

Her head tilted to one side. "No, this is what I had in mind all along."

"So what's stopping you?" As soon as the words left his mouth he regretted them. It wasn't like the crib was expensive, but maybe it was out of her budget.

"I'm not what you would call impulsive. I need to mull things over for a while."

"In case you haven't figured this out already, babies don't exactly afford one the luxury of mulling. They usually require snap decisions." He paused for a moment. "I have an idea. What if I got it for you? Combination Christmas *and* baby gift."

"You think I can't afford it, don't you?"

"No."

Arms crossed, she lifted a brow.

"Let's just say I wanted to remove any potential obstacles."

After another look at the crib, she said, "I suppose, since we came in your truck, this would be a good time to go ahead and pick it up."

"Yes, it would."

"However—" she held up an index finger "—I will purchase it myself. Thanks to the sale of my house and the fact that I'm not paying any rent, my finances are just fine."

"Then, I guess I'll just have to come up with another gift idea."

Her blue eyes met his. "Gabriel, your friendship is the greatest gift I could ever receive."

The reminder had his gut clenching.

"Looks like we'll need another cart," she said.

"No, we need an associate. You okay to look at baby stuff while I find someone?"

"Yes." She lifted her chin. "I'll be fine."

Annoyance nipped at his heels as he strode up the aisle. If he was such a good friend, why hadn't she confided in him all those months ago? Instead, she'd clammed up, turning her back on him without explanation. And it hurt more than he was willing to admit.

Chapter Seven

After a little more than a month in Grandmama's house, things were starting to feel like home. Jillian loved her new living room. The wood floors were beautiful, the wall color was just right for her furniture and the area rug from her old place helped bring the entire space together. While she'd held on to Grandmama's antique dining-room set, the fresh wall color paired with a new area rug livened up the space. Most surprising of all was that Jillian now had a nursery.

The white crib and Grandmama's old chest of drawers Gabriel had painted to match looked so nice against the palest of pink walls. Once Jillian added the quilted bedding set in shades of pink, white and gray she'd found online, the room looked like something out of a magazine.

And she owed it all to Gabriel. His little pep talk during their shopping trip almost two weeks ago was just the impetus she needed. He'd given her the courage and gentle prodding—not to mention help—she'd needed to get things in order. The look on his face when she'd done her big reveal last night had made her even more excited for the arrival of her yet-to-be-named daughter.

She'd contemplated Mae, in honor of Grandmama, but was also partial to Hannah. Then again, Hannahs were a dime a dozen these days. She'd even toyed with Eva and Clare, but neither of those felt right either.

With a sigh, she returned to her work at hand in the storage room of the youth barn Wednesday evening, thankful she still had almost a dozen weeks before she'd need to decide on that name.

She paused her tagging to look around the large space filled with all of the donations they'd received thus far. Quilts and throws, toys, gaming systems, movies, jewelry, even a couple of televisions. There were also several handcrafted items, including a Texas-themed firepit and an amazing wood-and-iron side table with an inlaid lone star she and Gabriel had picked up from a gentleman in Carmine. Gabriel liked it so much he'd asked the man for his contact info in case he wanted to order one.

Hmm. That might make a nice Christmas gift for Gabriel. After all he'd done for her, he deserved something special. She'd have to keep that in mind.

She paused to pet Aggie, who lay patiently at her feet. Thanks to her, Jillian had been feeling more like her old self these last couple of weeks. She hadn't had a panic attack in a while. A little trepidation at times, but no full-blown anxiety.

Spending time with Gabriel had helped, too. He'd been so good to her. Seemed they were together at some point almost every day, making it more and more difficult to keep her feelings in check. But what choice did she have? Gabriel would never be interested in her as anything more than a friend. Not only had she hurt him by pulling away without explanation, not trusting him enough to tell him the truth of what had happened to her, but he deserved better.

She moved on to the next table. So did Aggie. A rod suspended behind her held coats, jackets and other hanging items someone else was working on. From the sound of it, there were a couple of women on the opposite side. Which was good. They'd done their best to stay on top of things, sorting and tagging each week so they wouldn't have so much to do in the days leading up to the bazaar. Especially when they were expecting an influx of donations after Thanksgiving.

Jillian reached for a stack of children's clothing to begin tagging when she heard one of the two women mention her name.

She took a step back as one of them said, "I don't care if she is Ida Mae's granddaughter. An unmarried, pregnant woman has no business working with these kids. That's not the sort of example they need."

Jillian froze, her insides knotting. How many other people felt the same way that woman did? Sadly, there was a time Jillian would have said, or at least thought, the same thing. Judged someone without knowing their story.

And yet, while she firmly believed the child growing inside of her was a gift from God, she was afraid to tell people the truth behind it. Why was that? Was she going to live the rest of her life like that? And make her little girl feel inferior?

No. She had to find a way to let go of the shame that held her captive. For her sake and her baby's. But how? She'd talked to counselors. Read blogs and books. Yet she still carried this burden.

Eyeing her watch, she realized services would be ending soon, so she returned her marker and tags to the main table, took hold of Aggie's leash and went outside. They crossed the parking lot to the main church building, where she found Pastor Green and scheduled a meeting.

And the next morning, before the library

opened, she sat across from him at his desk in his office at the church and told him about her assault and her inability to break free of the disgrace.

Elbows perched on the arms of his desk chair, he steepled his fingers as he either pondered or tried to recover from everything she'd just thrown at him. "Jillian, do you believe God allows bad things to happen to good people? His people?"

"Yes, sir. These last few months I've often thought of Joseph."

"He's a perfect example. He was sold into slavery by his jealous brothers. Then, just when his life was looking up, he was falsely accused by Potiphar's wife."

"I know God has not forsaken me. I sense His guidance. But I can't help feeling as though I'm holding back when it comes to my baby. Because unlike most women, I don't have a husband or even a significant other." Lowering her head, she stared at the tissue in her hands. "I overheard someone say I was a bad example for the youth because I'm an unwed mother." She looked at him now. "I didn't choose either of those things."

"They were wrong to say that, Jillian."

"How do I deal with the truth, though? It's not something I can simply blurt out." She sighed. "I love my baby, and I'm going to keep her. But it's as though I'm harboring this big secret that's holding me captive to shame."

"Then, bring it out of the darkness and into the light."

She looked at him. "I'm sorry?"

"The thief comes to steal, kill and destroy. But Jesus came so you could have a full and abundant life, regardless of your circumstances."

Suddenly, she got it. "Yet I've been focused on myself and my circumstances instead of entrusting them to Jesus."

He rested his arms atop his desk. "Being a Christian doesn't shield us from the depravity of this fallen world. But because of our faith and the hope it brings, we can rise above our circumstances." He paused for a moment. "You know, Joseph is actually the focus of my message this Sunday. He's a good example of rising above one's circumstances."

"He did nothing, yet he was thrown into prison."

"'But the Lord was with Joseph and shewed him mercy and gave him favor in the sight of the keeper of the prison.'" Pastor Green paused. "Jillian, would you like to give your testimony as part of my sermon?"

She felt her eyes widen. "Why?"

"Twofold. First, you're a modern-day example of bad things happening to even the strongest believers. Second, and I believe most important, it would give you a platform to bring the truth to light and free yourself from that captivity you mentioned."

She released a long breath. "I understand what you're saying, but it's still a scary prospect."

"Scarier than being entrapped by your shame?"

"When you put it like that." After a slight hesitation, she said, "Can I pray on it?"

"Absolutely. That's the best thing you could do." He scribbled something on a piece of paper and handed it to her. "Here's my number. You can call or text me your decision." He stood and she followed suit, taking hold of the proffered card.

"Thank you for seeing me, Pastor. You've shifted my perspective. Joseph's a good example. I may have to read his story again. This time through a different lens."

She walked out of his office feeling lighter than she had in months. Though, she still had a big decision to make. Could she really stand up in front of the entire church and share the truth about her pregnancy?

She was definitely going to have to call in some prayer warriors on this one. And she knew just who. Two of them were at the Hope Crossing Senior Living Community, and the other lived right next door.

Doc had no desire to retire.

It had become painfully obvious after Gabriel

had suggested the man trim his schedule to four days a week, leaving him more time for those projects that were always waiting at home. Doc had shut him down faster than a cheetah with an adrenaline rush. Leaving Gabriel with little hope the man would retire anytime soon.

So as Gabriel locked up the clinic a little before five thirty Thursday afternoon, he was torn. He loved working in Hope Crossing where he'd grown up and knew everyone. But he was concerned about his future. If something happened to Doc, Gabriel feared he'd be gone, too. Not by choice, but because ownership of the clinic would fall to Doc's children, and they had no interest in their father's business. So what was to keep them from selling?

Gabriel's only hope would be to convince them to sell it to him. He had a nice nest egg and had invested wisely. But what if they wanted more than he could afford? Lately, a lot of small, privately owned clinics like Doc's were being scooped up by groups of doctors for outlandish prices. Prices that translated to higher cost of services. Something the people of Hope Crossing couldn't afford. Not to mention they'd lose that personal touch. A new doctor wouldn't know the Barnharts' donkey was feeling poorly because ol' Chester had gotten into Ms. Mazie's garden and some of her crops didn't agree with donkeys.

Gabriel would hate to see that happen. He had to think about his future, though. Should he be proactive and start exploring other options? But that could mean leaving Hope Crossing.

He'd contemplated doing just that earlier this year. But now?

You could give it to God.

He threw himself into his vet truck and started the engine. Seemed the more his concern grew, the harder it was to let go and let God. Yes, he believed God had a plan. Gabriel just wished he knew what it was.

The sun was setting when he pulled out of the clinic parking lot, and he wished he hadn't been so eager to complete all those projects at Jillian's. At least they'd given him something to focus on besides his own issues.

His phone rang, and Jillian's name appeared on the dashboard. "Hey, Jillian."

"Hey, yourself. What are you doing?"

"I just left the clinic."

"Are you available to swing by the assisted living? I have something I'd like to discuss with you and the grandmas."

"Is everything okay?"

"Yes. I need some input, though."

"I'm on my way. See you in a few." Curiosity had him pushing the speed limit. Jillian had been unusually quiet on the ride home from church last night. Yet while she'd said she had a lot on her mind, she hadn't elaborated.

Five minutes later, he arrived at the assisted living as Jillian, Aggie and the grandmas were leaving the dining room.

They continued to Ms. Ida Mae's room, where the grandmas sat on their walker seats, insisting Gabriel and Jillian take the recliner and easy chair in front of the window, separated by a small side table.

"Something's got you stirred up, Jilly." Ms. Ida Mae watched her granddaughter.

"Yes, though it's nothing bad." Leaning back, Jillian set one hand atop her rounded belly while the other rested on Aggie. "Last night at church I overheard someone commenting that I shouldn't be helping with the youth because as a single, pregnant woman I was a bad example."

The grandmas' gasps were audible, while Gabriel's body tensed.

"Any idea who it was?" Ms. Ida Mae asked.

Jillian shook her head. "I didn't recognize her voice."

"Some people are so quick to assume the worst," said Mamaw. "I'd like to tell them a thing or two." And Gabriel had no doubt she would, too.

While he remained silent, he shared his grandmother's frustration that someone would jump to conclusions like that. Especially in church. At the same time, he suddenly understood what Jillian had been saying about feeling as though she was keeping a secret.

"Their comments had me meeting with Pastor Green today."

"Good," said Mamaw. "Someone needs to stop that sort of talk."

The corners of Jillian's mouth tipped upward. "That's not why I went to see him. Their comments simply motivated me." Smoothing her hands over her jeans, she explained the reason for her visit with the pastor and said she'd told him the reality behind her pregnancy. "He gave me a lot to think about." She clasped her hands under her chin. "And asked me if I'd like to share my testimony with the church."

Gabriel recalled the way Jillian had struggled to explain things to him in Ms. Ida Mae's kitchen that night she arrived in Hope Crossing. "Are you sure you want to do that?"

"I wasn't at first. But Pastor's comment about bringing my secret out of the darkness and into the light has been with me all day. All these months, I've kept silent about the circumstances of my baby. I'm tired of hiding."

Silence reigned for a long moment. Aggie rested her head in Jillian's lap.

Meanwhile, Gabriel's insides churned. How

could Jillian stand before the church and tell the entire congregation what had happened to her when she hadn't even been able to tell him?

"Pastor gave you some sage advice," Mamaw finally said. "Secrets have a way of eating away at us. And they most certainly refuse to be ignored."

As his ire continued to grow, Gabriel could attest to that.

"That's why I need to do this," said Jillian. "I'm tired of lurking in the shadows. I want to step out into the light of truth. But I can't do it without your help."

"Of course, Jilly. Whatever you want us to do."

Jillian smiled. "I need you to pray for me. That the words that come out of my mouth won't be from me, but from God."

With assurances from the grandmas, Gabriel and Jillian made their way to their respective vehicles a short time later, Gabriel growing more frustrated with each step. He had questions that needed answers.

In the parking lot, he caught Jillian's gaze. "Could we talk at your place?"

"Sure. Have you eaten?"

"No." Not that he had an appetite.

While Jillian heated some soup on her stove a short time later, Gabriel watched from the opposite side of the counter, carefully formulating his words. Putting her on the defensive wouldn't get him anywhere.

"Do you remember Annalise and Hawkins's wedding?" That was when he'd first contemplated a move to Dallas.

Pink tinged her cheeks. "How could I forget?"

"So you can imagine how confused I was when, only a few weeks later, you suddenly wanted nothing to do with me."

Her movements stilled.

"Jillian, why didn't you tell me what happened to you?"

Her shoulders fell along with her gaze. "I was too ashamed."

"So you thought it would be better to say nothing?" He dragged his fingers through his hair, trying to temper the anger he'd kept buried but could no longer ignore. "I thought we had something special. We used to text or talk multiple times each day. And then you just cut me off. What was I supposed to think?"

"I'm sorry." Ignoring Aggie's offers of comfort, Jillian crossed her arms. "My mind was messed up."

"I could've been there for you. Helped you walk that road. But you never gave me the opportunity."

"I was afraid."

"Of what?"

"That you would look at me differently." Lowering her arms, she gave in to Aggie. "That you would quietly turn your back on me."

"Like you did with me?"

She glared at him.

He watched her, wondering if she ever even knew him. "I guess we'll never know, will we?"

The soup sizzled, boiling over.

Jillian turned off the heat and removed the pot from the burner. "It was never my intention to hurt you. If anything, I was trying to protect you."

He glared at her. "News flash. You *did* hurt me."

She sighed, her eyes closing as tears spilled onto her cheeks. Her sob tore at him, but he refused to bend.

Finally, she looked at him, fingers pressed to her quivering lips. "I'm sorry, Gabriel. So, so sorry."

He wanted to turn his back on her. To rush out the door, retreat to his house and lick his wounds. Find some way to justify his actions.

Then he saw his own pain reflected in Jillian's watery eyes.

They'd both lost something precious that awful day in May. Did he really want to cause her more pain?

"If that's how you felt," Jillian began, "why have you done so much for me now?"

"Because we were friends first. And that's what friends do."

"And now? Are we still friends? Can you forgive me for what I did?"

He sucked in a breath. Let it out. "Yes, Jillian. I forgive you."

Chapter Eight

Jillian awoke Sunday morning feeling more peace than she had in a long time. And while a small part of her worried how her testimony might be received—people thinking she was looking for sympathy or fabricating a story to make herself look better—she knew in her heart this was what she needed to do. Not only for herself, but for anyone listening who might be facing their own struggle.

The past few days she'd spent a lot of time in God's word, asking Him what He wanted her to say. Because the congregation was so varied—from elementary age kids to the grandmas—she needed to get her point across without going into detail. And after mulling things over, she was sure she'd be able to do that despite opting not to make any notes. She preferred to speak from her heart.

Yet as she walked into the sanctuary and looked toward the pulpit, doubt and insecurity threatened to steal her resolve. She couldn't let that happen. The pastor was counting on her. God was counting on her. And He would be with her when she took that stage.

She continued down the center aisle with Aggie on one side of her and Grandmama on the other while Gabriel and Ms. Milly followed. Nearing the second-row pew, she felt a hand on her elbow.

Turning, her gaze collided with Gabriel's. Though his confrontation Thursday night had only been a speed bump in their friendship, realizing her selfishness had caused him so much pain filled her with regret.

"You're going to do great. I believe in you."

She couldn't help smiling. After what she'd put him through, she didn't deserve his friendship. Yet here he was. "Thank you."

They slipped into the grandmas' usual pew. Their seating arrangement was the same as always, Jillian on one end, Gabriel on the other and the grandmas in between, except this time Jillian was seated at the end of the pew with Aggie so she could step out easily when the pastor called her.

Jillian took in the pumpkins and russet-, burnt-orange-and cream-colored mums that adorned the stage, realizing that by this time next week they'd be into the Christmas season. Not to mention, mere days away from the Christmas Bazaar.

She'd already offered to host Thanksgiving dinner for Gabriel and the grandmas and had gotten a turkey when she and Gabriel went shopping yesterday. Since they had to pick up another donation and both were in need of groceries, they'd decided to combine them into one trip. Which had actually been kind of fun. She learned that Gabriel had a strong dislike for anything cranberry, while he seemed surprised when she insisted stuffing should be made from scratch, not a box.

The outing had also calmed her fears, proving that, despite her actions, they were still friends.

"Jillian." She looked up to find Annalise smiling down at her.

Standing, she hugged her friend who'd announced earlier in the month that she was also pregnant. "How are you feeling?"

"Pretty good." Annalise held out an envelope. "Here is the certificate portion of the Christmas-tree farm's donation for the bazaar. Hawkins dropped the other stuff off at the youth barn, but I wanted to make sure this didn't get lost."

Thinking about the abundance of items stored in the barn, Jillian said, "Smart move." She accepted the envelope as the piano began to play.

"I'd better get back to my seat." Annalise gave her a quick hug. "We'll talk later."

Soon, the worship leader welcomed everyone before leading them in song. Then, after the offering, the pastor moved to the podium.

Jillian took a deep breath as Grandmama reached for her hand and gave it a squeeze.

After opening his Bible, the pastor said, "The title of my message today is 'Bad Things Happen to Good People.' If you would, please turn in your Bibles to Genesis, chapter thirty-seven." Gripping the edges of the podium, he scanned the congregation. "Today, I'd like to introduce you to a young man by the name of Joseph."

The pastor moved somewhat quickly through the part about Joseph's dreams and his brothers selling him into slavery, then he picked up again at the point where Joseph was falsely accused by Potiphar's wife and thrown into prison. "Sometimes we tend to think that if we're good Christians—reading our Bibles and going to church regularly—we're insulated from the outside world. That the horrible stuff we hear about on the news can't touch us. And while I wish that was the case, sadly, it is not. We are fallen people surrounded by other fallen people, and all of us are living in a fallen world. Just like Joseph.

"I'd like to pause here and ask one of our newest members to share her testimony." He glanced

Jillian's way, causing her pulse to race. "Jillian, would you come up here, please?"

With Aggie at her side, she slipped out of the pew into the aisle, her heart pounding as she put one foot in front of the other until she was beside the pastor. Taking her place at the podium, she instructed Aggie to sit. Then, standing tall, chin up and shoulders squared, Jillian looked out at the congregation.

Suddenly her jitters were gone, replaced by peace. The kind that could only come from above.

"Hello. My name is Jillian McKenna. I'm sure many of you are familiar with my grandmother, Ida Mae Crowley." She smiled Grandmama's way. "And some of you have probably watched me grow up since I'd often visit her from Dallas and have been coming to church with her since I was a little girl. However, as of a few weeks ago, I am now a proud resident of Hope Crossing, serving as the town's new library director. Something I never would've imagined until recently."

A brief round of applause ensued.

As the room again fell silent, she drew in a deep breath, one hand going to Aggie's head. Digging her fingers into the soft fur, she continued. "Like many of you, I grew up in the church. And at the age of nine, I accepted Jesus as my Savior and was baptized. I went to a Christian college. I trust God and have a personal relationship with Him. And my life, for the most part, has gone relatively smoothly. Until this past May."

She briefly told the congregation of her passion for jogging and her decision to run alone that day. And when she saw the grandmas dabbing their unshed tears with tissues, she promptly averted her gaze.

Lifting her chin a notch higher, Jillian continued. "On that beautiful spring morning, my world was rocked by an unimaginable event that stole my confidence, left me terrified and filled me with more shame than I ever imagined. Weeks later, I learned I was pregnant. The news brought me to my knees and, again, had me asking God why.

"Then I heard my baby's heartbeat. For as long as I can remember, I've wanted to be a mother. And while I never would've dreamed it would happen this way, there it was. The desire of my heart. Out of that terrible, horrific event, God had given me beauty for ashes. Or as Joseph told his brothers, what was intended for evil, God used for good."

She scanned the congregation once again. "Life doesn't always go the way we think it will. As believers, we aren't promised a life free of pain and suffering. Just ask Joseph. But God does promise that He will never leave us nor forsake us. Even in the worst of times.

"I once heard someone say every one of us is either coming out of a trial, in the midst of a trial or about to go into one. Wherever you may be, no matter how deep your pain is, God is still with you, even though you might feel as though you've been forgotten. And like Joseph, you *can* choose to rise above your circumstances, trusting that God is at work and has a plan for your life."

Jillian's hand moved from Aggie to her belly. "My little girl is due to arrive in February. And while it may not be the perfect scenario I always imagined, she's a gift, nonetheless. And like it says in the book of James, *every* good and perfect gift is from above. Thank you."

To her surprise, people rose to their feet and began to applaud. Loudly.

Overcome, her hand again fell to Aggie as the pastor gave her a sideways shoulder hug.

"Well done, Jillian," he said against her ear. "You spoke from your heart."

She nodded and started toward her seat much faster than she'd made her way onto the stage, for fear she'd lose it in front of all these people.

Thankfully, Grandmama met her with a fresh tissue and a hug. "I'm so proud of you."

As Jillian took her seat, peace flooded through her. She felt like a prisoner set free. And perhaps that was what had happened. By bringing her shame to light, it had lost its hold on her.

Oh, how she prayed so.

Gabriel caught himself whistling a Christmas song as he strolled through the clinic late Monday morning. No wonder the staff looked at him like his head was screwed on backward. What could he say? Things were finally looking up. Doc had come to him earlier saying he was considering cutting his schedule to only four days, Gabriel and Jillian had finally cleared the air, and yesterday had marked what he hoped was the beginning of Jillian's healing.

It took guts for a person to get up in front of the entire church and share their testimony. But given the sensitive nature of Jillian's story, Gabriel's admiration was tenfold. He'd never forget the look on her face when she descended those steps. For the first time since she'd moved to Hope Crossing, she looked at peace. She looked…like the old Jillian. The one who'd stolen his heart and had him contemplating a move to Dallas.

His phone buzzed on his hip, interrupting his reverie. Removing it from its clip, he slipped into his office to glance at the screen. The youth minister?

"Hey, Ricky. What's up?"

"Gabriel." The man sighed. "I'm afraid I've got some bad news." Why did he sound so grim?

Gabriel hoped something hadn't happened to Ricky's wife. "Go ahead."

"The youth barn was broken into last night. The storage area."

"What? How? Wasn't it locked?"

"Someone cut the lock." Another sigh filtered through the line. "The donations. Everything is gone."

Gabriel dropped into the leather chair, feeling as though he'd been kicked in the gut. "Why?"

"Who knows? Probably someone looking for a way to make some quick cash."

"But how would they know the stuff was there?" He shoved his fingers through his hair.

"We've been requesting donations all over the place. Wouldn't be difficult for someone to put two and two together."

"You don't suppose it was an inside job, do you?"

"That crossed my mind. I pray that's not the case, though."

Gabriel hoped so, too. "Is there anything I can do?"

"That's kind of why I'm calling. Could I get you to break the news to Ms. Milly and Ms. Ida Mae?"

Gabriel cringed. The two of them had worked

tirelessly to organize the event and acquire donations. They were excited, and it had given them a sense of purpose. Telling them was going to be like telling a kid there'd be no presents at Christmas.

But he knew Ricky had his hands full right now. "Yeah, I can do that." He just didn't know when. "Have you said anything to Jillian?"

"I was hoping you might tell her, too. Perhaps you two could tell your grandmothers together."

Probably not a bad idea. He glanced at his watch. It was almost lunchtime. "Are you going to be at the church for a while?"

"Oh, yeah. I'm not going anywhere anytime soon."

"I'll see if Jillian's available, and we'll head your way shortly."

One of the techs poked her head into his office as he ended the call. "Your next appointment is here."

His last one before lunch. Thankfully, it was only a canine-wellness exam, so he should be able to break away as soon as he was done.

"Tell them I'll be right there." Then he typed out a quick text to Jillian.

Could you break away in about thirty minutes? There's something that requires our immediate attention.

A second later, a dancing bubble appeared in the corner of the screen.

That sounds rather ominous. But yes, I can break away.

He quickly typed I'll explain when I get there.

Thirty-one minutes later, he pulled into the parking lot of the single-story brick building that housed not only the library but the fire station and town hall, as well. By the time he'd parked, Jillian was out the door with Aggie at her side and moving toward his truck.

He hopped out to meet her. The midday air was cool, and a slight breeze added a chill.

"What's going on?" Her brow creased in question.

"Ricky called me a little while ago. There was a break-in at the church. The youth barn, specifically. The donations are gone."

Her eyes widened. "What?"

"I told him I'd meet him over there. Thought you might like to go with me."

She nodded. "Let's go."

He rattled off the rest of his conversation with Ricky as they made the short drive, including the part about telling the grandmas.

"They worked so hard," Jillian said as they

pulled into the church parking lot. "This is going to break their hearts."

"My thoughts exactly." He continued toward the back of the property and the metal building where a couple of sheriff's vehicles were parked.

Moments later, he and Jillian exited his truck and walked toward the side of the building where a roll-up door sat open to the space that only yesterday had brimmed with donations of every type. And as they approached the opening and peered inside, Gabriel's heart sank.

Save for the upended tables and a few items of clothing littering the floor, the space was empty. And as if to punctuate their work, the thieves had spray-painted a few choice words on the walls.

For perhaps the first time ever, he was at a loss. The guy who was used to helping suddenly found himself clueless. So much stuff. Gone. Right along with the kids' dreams of a mission trip.

Turning, he saw Aggie licking Jillian's hand. Meanwhile, Jillian's gaze darted about the space. Her face was pale, and her chin had a slight tremble.

He started to reach for her but feared startling her. And he couldn't help wondering what was going on inside her head. The same feelings of disgust he felt? Or something much more personal?

He stepped closer. "Jillian?"

With a shake of her head, she dug her fingers into Aggie's fur.

"Gabriel!"

They both turned as Ricky and Brady James, a sheriff's deputy and a member of Gabriel's Sunday-school class, approached. They gave him and Jillian a brief rundown of what they suspected had happened. Though a single statement from Brady pretty much summed things up.

"The likelihood of recovering any of the items is slim. Even if we did find anything, there'd be no way to prove it came from here."

Jillian cleared her throat. "So what are we supposed to do? What about the bazaar?"

Ricky shook his head. "I don't know. I mean, it's not like we can go back to folks and ask them to donate again." Hands buried in the pockets of his jeans, he shrugged. "I really hate this, guys. The kids were so excited. Your grandmothers had them energized and believing they could earn enough money for their trip. Now the rug's been pulled out from under them. I don't know how I'm going to tell them."

"I doubt you'll need to," said Brady. "You know how news travels around here. Once word gets out—if it hasn't already—everyone's gonna know."

"You're right about that." Gabriel turned his attention to Jillian, who still looked stunned. "That means we need to tell the grandmas right away. Because if we don't, they're apt to hear it from someone else."

After another glance into the now-empty space, Jillian nodded. "We should go."

"Okay." Wondering what her abruptness was about, he addressed the men. "Let me know if you have any news."

Jillian stared straight ahead as they returned to his truck, one hand fisted around Aggie's leash while the other was buried in the pocket of her cardigan. With her hair pulled up, he could see her jaw clench and unclench. Her nostrils flare.

He hated to see her so upset. Especially after yesterday.

Moving to open her door, he said her name.

Her only response was "We need to hurry." She climbed into the truck and remained silent until he pulled out of the parking lot. Then it was as if a dam had broken.

"It's bad enough to steal from a church. But to steal from a bunch of kids!" Vehemence laced her tone. "What kind of person does that? All they wanted to do was fund their mission trip. Yet some thugs come along and strip that ability away from them." She let out a guttural roar that seemed to surprise Aggie as much as Gabriel. "Crime happens in large cities. *Not* in Hope Crossing. That's why I moved here. So to see these kids touched by this sort of evil sickens me. How are they supposed to bounce back from this, Gabriel? And it's not just the kids. Our grandmothers are going to be devastated."

"I don't know about *devastated.* Saddened. Angry perhaps." Though probably not as angry as Jillian. He'd never seen this side of her.

"There's got to be something we can do," she said. "Some way to move forward with the bazaar."

He turned onto a side street. "How are we going to do that without anything to sell?"

"Everyone's been saying that this coming weekend would likely bring in a large amount of donations."

"Large in comparison, but not enough to make the bazaar worth the effort."

Nonetheless, Jillian released a sigh that was anything but defeated as he pulled up to the senior living. "My attacker took so many things from me. I refuse to allow these kids to endure that same sense of loss. Somehow we have to find a way to give them beauty for ashes."

In that moment, he understood her anger was coming out of her own experience.

He shifted his truck into Park before turning to face her. "I don't know how we're going to do that, but prayer would be a good place to start."

She nodded.

"And may I just say, righteous indignation looks very good on you, Jillian McKenna."

"It feels kind of good, too. Though, I meant every word of it."

"I have no doubt. Which means we've got work to do. Starting with breaking the news to the grandmas."

Chapter Nine

Jillian had no idea how to revive the bazaar after those crooks took everything, but she was determined to find a way.

She had to hand it to the grandmas. They'd taken the news about the theft much better than she had. The entire mess had stirred a fire inside of her. A fierce determination not to let the thieves win. Something good was going to come from this awful turn of events. She believed it in her heart and had been praying ever since.

So by Tuesday afternoon, she was feeling more hopeful. Gloriana Broussard, a mom of one of the girls in the youth group and a former television personality who was heavily involved in promoting the town's annual fair and rodeo, had met with Gabriel, Jillian and the grandmas last night to share an idea she hoped would bring in enough donations to make up for what had been stolen.

Then this morning, Gloriana took to the airwaves of at least three radio stations from Houston to Bryan–College Station to Austin, where she shared about the event that had been the brainchild of two grandmothers with a desire to help the youth and the devastating blow they'd suffered at the hands of some Scrooge-hearted thieves. She'd also included contact information for the church. Now they waited to see if people would be touched enough to respond to their plea.

How Jillian prayed they'd receive enough donations to allow them to proceed. She wasn't sure she could bear seeing the long faces on the kids. Not when they'd been so hopeful and excited.

Returning her focus to the computer screen in her office, she again attempted to concentrate on the order she'd been trying to place for some new reading materials.

Righteous indignation looks very good on you.

Her cheeks heated at the memory of Gabriel's words. Why that man wasn't married had to be the mystery of the century. Yes, he was handsome, but he was also kind, tenderhearted, compassionate and every other good trait one could possibly think of. If only things could've turned out differently for them.

But it was too late now. Not only had she hurt him, she was carrying a stranger's baby. End of story.

She scanned the page once again, making sure everything was as it should be, then clicked the submit button as someone knocked on her open office door.

She looked up to see her assistant smiling. "Someone is here to see you."

Jillian's gaze drifted to the window that allowed her to keep tabs on what was happening inside the library. That's when she spotted Gloriana holding her infant son.

"Thank you, Lucy."

Standing, Jillian went to greet the woman who was also Annalise's sister-in-law. "Gloriana, I wasn't expecting to see you." Her gaze fell to the baby boy in her arms. "He's so cute. How old?"

"He just turned four months." Gloriana smiled like any proud mother. "It won't be long, and you'll be toting around your own little one. You're having a girl, right?"

"Yes." Jillian's hand went to her abdomen. "I can't wait to meet her."

"I've been meaning to tell you how much I admire what you did Sunday. You are quite an inspiration."

Jillian shrugged. "We never know how our story might help someone else."

"This is true." Gloriana shifted the dark-haired babe to her other arm. "I received a phone call a little while ago from a television station in Houston. Someone there heard one of my spots this morning, and they'd like to interview Ms. Ida Mae and Ms. Milly, along with you and Gabriel."

"Why?"

"Because in the world of television, what happened here has all the makings of a great human-interest story. A couple of sweet grandmothers helping a group of teens achieve their goal only to have their efforts thwarted by a band of thieves. Throw in the fact that the holidays are upon us, and it's the sort of tale that'll tug at people's heartstrings and boost ratings. But they need an answer right away because they'd like to do the interview tomorrow morning."

"That doesn't give us much time to think about it." Though, after what she did Sunday, this would be nothing for Jillian. But what about everyone else?

"No, it doesn't. So I was hoping you could contact the involved parties and let me know so I can call the station back."

"That shouldn't be a problem. Though, I don't know how soon I'll get a response from Gabriel. It just depends how busy he is."

"I understand." Gloriana gave Jillian her number, then departed while Jillian began contacting the others, starting with a text to Gabriel to call her ASAP.

Back in her office, she dialed Grandmama.

Once the woman had her phone on Speaker with Ms. Milly, Jillian relayed the information Gloriana had shared.

"This could give us just the boost we need, Jilly. Two old ladies pleading for donations for a bunch of youngsters." Grandmama chuckled. "Folks won't be able to resist."

"Grandmama!"

"Oh, lighten up, Jilly. You know it's true."

She shook her head. "You don't have to sound so manipulative."

"Don't you worry, Jillian," said Ms. Milly. "I'll be sure to keep her in line."

Jillian's phone beeped, indicating an incoming call. After a quick glance at the screen she said, "I need to take this. It's Gabriel."

"All right, Jilly. Tell him Milly and I are both on board for this."

"Yes, ma'am. Talk to you soon." She quickly switched calls. "Gabriel."

"What's up? It sounded urgent."

She relayed the information about the interview. "The grandmas are in favor of doing it. What about you?"

"Doesn't bother me." He hesitated a moment. "How do you feel about it?"

She appreciated that he asked. "I think it's something that could lead to even more donations. So I say *yes*."

"In that case, tell Gloriana to roll with it."

Hope swelled inside of Jillian. "I will."

"Before I let you go, Ricky texted me a little while ago. Seems the phones at the church have been ringing off the hook since they came in this morning. People who heard Gloriana and wanted to know how they could help."

"I hope that translates into some donations. We have a lot of inventory to replenish."

By the time she said goodbye, Jillian was so excited she barely managed any work the rest of the day. Except asking her assistant if she could manage things tomorrow morning while Jillian was at the assisted living.

Since the reporter had informed Gloriana that she and her camera operator would arrive around nine Wednesday morning, Jillian made sure she was there by eight thirty. Gabriel had a surgery scheduled first thing, so he was a few minutes behind her. And by the time the reporter and cameraperson arrived, Gloriana was there, too.

And once the camera started rolling, the grandmas spoke from their hearts.

"Just because we're in assisted living and have a harder time getting around doesn't mean we're useless," said Grandmama. "So long as we're able, we have a responsibility to guide the younger generations."

When they were ready for Gabriel and Jillian,

butterflies threatened to get the best of her. But as soon as she thought about the kids, her anxiety vanished. Because this wasn't about her or Gabriel or even the grandmas. This was about the kids and their desire to share the good news of Jesus with others.

"All right," the female reporter said as they packed up a short time later. "We're going to get this edited so we can have it ready for tonight's newscast. This is just the kind of story people like to see as we head into the holidays. Hopefully, some of our viewers will reach out and help you all make up for the things those grinches stole."

Gabriel smiled. "We appreciate the opportunity. Who knows what'll come of it? But whatever happens, God's got a plan."

Once the television people left, Gabriel and Jillian said their goodbyes so they could get back to work.

"What are you doing tonight?" Gabriel held the front door for her.

She stepped into the cold, windy air, hugging her jacket a little tighter. "Prepping for Thanksgiving tomorrow."

"In all the chaos, I almost forgot about Thanksgiving. Anything I can help you with?"

A thrill shot through her, but she promptly reined it in. Gabriel was always eager to lend a helping hand. "If you like."

"And we'll have to watch the news so we can see how things turned out." His phone rang. "It's Ricky." He held the device to his ear. "What's up, Ricky?" He paused. "Right now?" He glanced at his watch. "Jillian's with me. I guess we can spare a couple of minutes." He looked at her now, eyebrows lifted in question.

She nodded.

"Okay, we'll be right there." Ending the call, he looked at her. "Ricky says he's got something he wants to show us."

Shivering as they continued toward the parking lot, Jillian said, "I'll see you there."

Five minutes later, they entered the back of the church, near the offices.

Moments later, Ricky appeared. "Come with me."

They followed him down the hall to one of the Sunday-school rooms.

"We've had a lot of visitors this morning," he said.

"Oh?" Jillian sent Gabriel a questioning look as Ricky flipped on the light.

Inside the space, there were two beanbag chairs, a wide assortment of toys, some small appliances and a couple of Blu-ray players.

"People have been dropping off stuff all morning." Ricky's smile could hardly be contained. "Including cash and a couple of checks."

Jillian giggled. "This is amazing."

"Every one of the donors said they'd heard about our plight on the radio."

"Thank you, Gloriana," said Gabriel. "Sounds like we should make some arrangements for this weekend, then, because we and the grandmas just finished an interview with a television station out of Houston and they're planning to air it tonight." He scanned the space. "If this is any indication, we might find ourselves with a deluge of donations."

With an unexpected giddiness bubbling inside of her, Jillian said, "Library's closed Friday, so I'll be happy to come up here."

"Clinic's closed, too," said Gabriel. "So count me in."

Ricky smiled. "In that case, I'll make some phone calls. See if any of the kids would like to help."

"Sounds like the bazaar is back on." And it might end up being bigger than any of them had imagined.

By Friday, there was someone at the church around the clock. And it hadn't been solely Gabriel's idea. Several men from the church had stepped up to make sure the revived bazaar would not be compromised. Some offered to accept late-night deliveries while others pledged to guard the donations.

Gabriel and Jillian had arrived at the youth barn at seven Friday morning and stayed until almost seven that night as a steady stream of cars and trucks rolled through to drop off a wide variety of items for the bazaar, cash and enough food to feed a small army. Though the latter had been the favorite of the teenage boys who'd come to help.

Yet despite the renewed enthusiasm, the daylong vigil meant Jillian wasn't able to partake in the one thing she had been looking forward to most—searching for and cutting down a Christmas tree.

So Gabriel decided to make sure that happened.

After verifying there would be enough people at the church Saturday morning, he contacted Annalise and Hawkins about a private tree-selection time. Annalise had been more than happy to oblige. Even if it meant Hawkins had to be on the tractor before eight Saturday morning to drive them into the maze of trees at the Hope Crossing Christmas Tree Farm.

"Where are you going?" Perched in the passenger seat of his pickup just after seven thirty Saturday morning, Jillian appeared rather indignant when he turned right instead of left coming out of their neighborhood. "This isn't the way to the church."

"That's because we're not going to the church." He managed a matter-of-fact tone, despite the excitement zinging through him.

"But what about donations? We have so much tagging to do between now and next Saturday. You are aware that the bazaar is only a week from today?"

One arm draped atop the steering wheel, he stared straight ahead, trying to hide his amusement. "Yes, I am. And there are people at the church waiting to do all of that."

"So where are *we* going?"

"You'll find out." In the rearview mirror he noticed Aggie in the back seat, seemingly trying to keep up with their conversation.

Hoping to calm Jillian down, he turned on the radio, and Christmas music filled the space between them. If nothing else, it would set the mood.

She continued to glare at him. "I don't know what you've got up your sleeve, but I hope I don't have to tattle on you to Ms. Milly."

Making another right, he almost laughed out loud. Mamaw and Ms. Ida Mae had been in on his plan from the beginning. "Go right ahead."

Jillian was animated, to say the least. The robbery had really struck a chord with her. And her determination to see the bazaar go on despite the setback was to be admired. A far cry from the woman who'd been a shell of herself less than two months ago. And he enjoyed seeing this livelier version again.

"You can knock off the indignant act any time, Jillian. So things aren't happening the way you expected. Maybe you should learn to roll with it."

She leaned back against her seat. "I've had enough unexpected events for one year, thank you very much."

He couldn't argue that. "Point taken. But I thought you trusted me."

She grew quiet then, staring out the window at the countryside until Aggie rested her chin on Jillian's shoulder.

Reaching up to rub Aggie, Jillian said, "I'm sorry, Gabriel. I do trust you. It's just—"

"Ever heard the term *pleasantly surprised*?"

"Yes." She dragged the single word out.

"Then, trust me." He glanced her way. "Please?"

"All right." She returned her hands to her lap. "Can you give me a hint, though?"

Eyeing a handful of Black Angus huddled around a bale of hay, he shook his head and puffed out a laugh. "Okay, fine. It's someplace you've been talking about for weeks."

"Hmm. Well, it can't be the tree farm. They don't open until nine."

"That's too bad." That is, unless you knew the right people. Thankfully, he did.

"Wait," she finally said. "I recognize this. The tree farm *is* on this road."

He willed himself to remain calm. "Yes, it is."

"But they're not open yet."

The corners of his mouth lifted. "Oh, really?"

"Yes—wait. Gabriel, what did you do?" Her face lit with a mixture of surprise and delight.

"Scheduled a private appointment at the tree farm." He could feel her staring at him.

"Why?"

"Because you've been looking forward to it. And then we got busy waiting on donations." He sighed. "I didn't want things to get away from us and you end up disappointed."

She fell silent for a long moment while notes of "Have Yourself a Merry Little Christmas" filled the cab. "You did that for me?"

As if there wasn't much he wouldn't do for her. "Without hesitation."

Pulling into the drive at the Hope Crossing Christmas Tree Farm, he heard a sniffle from the passenger seat. "Thank you."

"You're welcome."

Soon, they'd traded the warmth of his truck for the brisk morning air. Thankfully, Jillian had been planning to stand outside to accept donations, so she was dressed appropriately.

As promised, Hawkins was waiting. "So what size are you thinking?"

"I don't know." Holding Aggie's leash, Jillian shrugged, her nose pink. "Seven, maybe eight feet."

"A seven-footer would probably be best." Gabriel looked at her. "I'm afraid an eight-footer would overwhelm your living room."

She nodded. "Good point."

"Leyland Cypress or Virginia pine?" Hawkins asked.

Gabriel deferred to Jillian.

"Pine."

"All right, then." Hawkins started toward the tractor. "Hop aboard the flatbed, and we'll be on our way."

In no time, the two of them were strolling among the rows of trees with Aggie, discussing the pros and cons of each one.

After moving up and down a couple of sections, Jillian said, "I can't decide. I like the fullness of this one. But the shape isn't quite as perfect as the one I saw back there." With Aggie looking up at her, she pointed to the previous row.

Gabriel stepped in front of her, armed with the saw Hawkins had given them. After setting it on the ground, he took hold of Jillian's hands. "I want you to close your eyes."

One brow lifted momentarily before she finally complied.

"I want you to envision your perfect tree."

She took a deep breath, like an actor getting into character. "Okay."

"Now, keeping your eyes closed, tell me what it looks like."

After a long moment, she relaxed. The corners of her mouth curled upward. "It's not perfectly shaped. A little fluffier at the bottom. A couple of gaps here and there where the snow collected."

Snow? Not likely in this part of Texas.

Still, he scrutinized every tree in his line of vision, searching for what she'd described. Finally, he spotted it.

He picked up the saw again. Then, not wanting to alarm Jillian, he said, "I want you to keep your eyes closed, and I'm going to put my arm around your waist." He snugged her close. "Now walk with me." Their movements were completely in sync. She fit perfectly against him, and her sweet fragrance coupled with the aroma of the trees teased his senses.

Aggie kept pace with them until they stopped in front of the tree he felt she'd described.

"Okay, you can open your eyes."

When she did, Jillian was silent for a long while. Then she began to blink rapidly. "This is exactly what was in my head." She looked up at him now. "How did you do that?"

"I listened to what you wanted. Then searched until I found it. Because you deserve nothing less than your heart's desire, Jillian."

The way she stared up at him, the wonder in her blue eyes, had him longing to make every dream she'd ever had come true.

Seconds ticked by. Their breath mingled in the cold morning air.

And then she took a step back and shoved her hands into the pockets of her peacoat. "So what do we do now?"

"If this is the tree you want, then we cut it down." He gestured to the saw.

"It's definitely the one." Her eyes glimmered as she bit her bottom lip. "Can I try cutting it?"

"Of course."

She dropped Aggie's leash.

After some quick instruction, Gabriel reached through the limbs to hold on to the trunk while she began to saw.

"It's working." The childlike lilt in her voice made him chuckle.

"Keep going."

"Almost there."

He held tighter, leaning it ever so slightly until he felt it break free.

"I did it." Scrambling to her feet, she did a little dance. "I cut down my first Christmas tree."

"Here." Setting the trunk on the ground, he nodded toward the tree. "Hold on to it so I can get your picture."

She dropped the saw and reached into the tree. "Come here, Aggie." The dog complied, and once Jillian had a good grip on it, Gabriel stepped back to take her picture.

"We need one of all of us," she said.

"I don't know if my arm is that long, but we'll give it a try." He moved to the opposite side of the tree and held out the phone. "Smile." He snapped a couple of selfies.

"Let me see." After all Jillian had been through, to see her so happy and carefree did his heart good.

Slightly winded, she said, "What do we do now?"

He took hold of the tree and eased it to the ground. "I'll text Hawkins to let him know we're ready. He'll pick us up, along with our tree, then the tree will be shaken to remove any debris, baled and then we take it back to your place."

She winced. "Do we have to decorate it right away?"

"Only if you want to. Otherwise, we can leave it in a bucket of water on your porch until you're ready."

"I feel like we should be at the church."

"I anticipated as much." Which was why he already had a bucket waiting back at his house.

"Maybe we could decorate it tonight." The pink in her cheeks deepened. "I mean, if you'd like to help me, that is."

"Of course. Besides, there's no way I'm going to let you carry this bad boy into the house and set it up by yourself."

She took hold of his arm and smiled at him. "I can't believe you arranged all of this just for me." Then she pushed up on her toes and kissed his cheek. "Thank you, Gabriel."

The simple gesture took him by surprise. And sparked to life feelings he'd been trying to ignore. Where was a fire extinguisher when you needed it?

Chapter Ten

Busy did not begin to describe the days since Jillian had cut down her Christmas tree. And if it hadn't been for Gabriel, she wouldn't have done that. He had to be the most thoughtful person she'd ever known. Even though she'd hurt him.

Recognizing she was too consumed with bazaar stuff to worry about a tree and then making special arrangements and driving her to the tree farm himself was enough to make any girl swoon. But when he'd suggested she describe her perfect tree and then actually found it for her? She'd been ready to throw her arms around his neck and kiss him like she'd never kissed anyone before.

Thankfully, she'd exercised a measure of restraint and settled for a simple kiss on his cheek.

After dropping the tree off at her house, they'd gone to the church, where they found a line of cars with people dropping off donations for the bazaar. The contributions had continued throughout the day, meaning she and Gabriel were too exhausted when they got home to even think about the tree.

Sunday was a different story, though. After church and lunch with the grandmas, Gabriel had brought the tree inside and set it up in the living room, right in front of the window, the way Grandmama had always done. Then they'd strung the lights.

Oh, who was she kidding? Gabriel had done them all by himself. Since all she'd ever known was a prelit tree, she was more of a hindrance than a help, so while he did the lights, she made a batch of cookies for them to enjoy as they hung the ornaments.

She loved the pretty glow of the lights. And the fragrance of the fresh Virginia pine was an added treat. But the fun they'd had while decorating left her longing for a deeper relationship with him. She couldn't do that to Gabriel, though. He deserved more. A better woman without baggage.

Since Monday, though, their sole focus, aside from work, had been the bazaar. With only days left to prepare, it had been all-hands-on-deck every night this week. While most of the items had been sorted as they came in, everything still had to be tagged. And if they waited until Friday, they'd never finish in time.

Jillian liked seeing the renewed excitement on the kids' faces. Now when they showed up, they were ready to work. The outpouring of love this past week had been a wonderful opportunity for them to experience the goodness of mankind and the joy of giving. It had been a good reminder for her, too.

Now as she sat in one of the classrooms with Ms. Milly Wednesday evening, tagging the over-abundance of smaller items—things like books, jewelry, kitchen utensils, pen sets and more—while laughter and Christmas music drifted from the gymnasium-size space where they were setting up tables and working on the overall layout for the bazaar, she thanked God for allowing her to be a part of this once-in-a-lifetime event.

"I'm kind of surprised Grandmama wasn't interested in tagging these books."

Ms. Milly paused her humming of "Jingle Bell Rock." "I'm not. She's had her sights set on those big-ticket items."

And there was a surprising number of them. Televisions, laptops, a go-kart, even a full-size air hockey table.

"Her and Gabriel," said Jillian. "He's had his eye on some gaming device."

Ms. Milly chuckled. "You know what they say. *The only difference between men and boys is the price of their toys.*"

Jillian nodded, adding a price tag to a *The Lord of the Rings* box set. "This is true. My father is all about golf gear, while my brother has more fishing poles than there are people in our family."

As notes of "White Christmas" began to play in the larger room, Ms. Milly peered at Jillian over the top of her glasses. "You know, my grandson is quite fond of you, Jillian."

Her heart stuttered as she set the books aside. While there was a time she would have believed that, things were different now. "We're just friends, Ms. Milly. And that's all we will ever be."

The older woman looked up from the boxed earring-and-necklace set she was marking. "Why do you say that, dear?"

"Isn't it obvious?" Jillian gestured to her belly. "I'm pregnant with another man's child. A stranger, at that." When people in her own family had voiced concerns about her decision to keep her baby, how could she expect Gabriel or any other man to accept her little girl?

"Do you think it's impossible for a man—the right man—to love a child that isn't his? After all, what happened isn't the child's fault."

Jillian reached for a stack of children's books. "When you put it like that… No, I suppose it's not impossible. But I'm the other half of that equation."

"I see." Gabriel's grandmother grabbed a velvet box containing a pair of cubic zirconia studs. "You don't feel you're worthy of love, is that it?"

The woman had hit the nail on the head. "It's hard to explain, but I feel…tainted."

"Look at me, child." There was an adamance in Ms. Milly's tone Jillian had rarely heard.

She lifted her gaze to find Ms. Milly's brown eyes boring into her. "I did, too."

What?

"I know just what you're going through, Jillian. Feeling tainted and ashamed."

What was Ms. Milly trying to say? "Why would you feel that way?"

"For the same reason as you. Except I was acquainted with the young man."

Gabriel's grandmother had been assaulted? "Oh, Ms. Milly."

The woman sat rigid, her hands clasped. "He was one of my father's hired hands. A handsome fellow who recognized I was sweet on him and wasn't afraid to take advantage of that. I was so ashamed. I blamed myself for flirting with him."

"That didn't give him the right to—"

"I know, child. But you know as well as I do how hard we can be on ourselves."

Jillian nodded, all too aware.

"I was fresh out of high school, so when my parents learned I was pregnant, they sent me to live with my aunt Gladys. She was a spinster who lived in Dallas. I was to stay there until I had the baby and then put it up for adoption. Then I would return to Hope Crossing as though nothing had ever happened. There was just one problem."

"What was that?" Jillian hung on the woman's every word.

"I didn't want to give up my baby."

"So what did you do?" Jillian thought no one else could possibly understand what she'd been through or how she felt. But Ms. Milly had understood all along.

"Well, while I was there, God placed this wonderful man in my path. He was seven years my senior and worked for Gladys, helping her around the house. He was very kind, always looking out for my well-being, as well as my aunt's. She'd known him since he was a little boy and trusted him." Milly smiled wistfully, seemingly lost in another time and place. "He was easy to talk to. Always kept his distance, though, afraid he might scare me. As our feelings for each other grew, he asked me to marry him, because he knew I wanted to keep my baby. He said he loved me and my child, regardless of whose it was, because he or she was a part of me."

Jillian cocked her head, feeling as though she was watching a movie as this love story unfolded. "Did you believe him?"

"I wanted to, but I was afraid. What if he changed his mind? What if he found he couldn't love my baby after all?"

Knowing all too well what Ms. Milly meant, Jillian said, "What did you do?"

Gabriel's grandmother chuckled. "I told my aunt what he'd said. And after she insisted I'd be hard-pressed to find a better man, I gave in to my heart and married him."

Jillian felt her eyes grow wide.

"That baby is Gabriel's father."

Chill bumps erupted down Jillian's arms. "Does Gabriel know this? And Grandmama?"

"Oh, yes. Ida Mae was the first person to know about the assault. She was my rock. And as far as Gabriel, my story is common knowledge in our family. Howard and I had a great love story." She covered Jillian's hand with her own. "Love has no boundaries, Jillian. No *if only*s or *what-if*s. True love transcends our pasts, our hurts and our circumstances. But there is one thing you have to do."

"What's that?"

"Be willing to accept it."

"How are things going in here?" Gabriel strolled into the room, startling Jillian.

Without missing a beat, Ms. Milly said, "Quite well." She looked up then. "I believe we're almost finished."

"A couple of the ladies brought some home-made candies and cookies," he said, "if you'd like to take a break."

Ms. Milly pushed out of her chair and reached for her walker. "Homemade candies and cookies are two of my favorite things this time of year." She started toward the door. "Hopefully, there'll still be some left by the time I get there." With a chuckle she disappeared out the door.

"How about you?" Gabriel peered down at Jillian. "I think I saw some fudge on one of the platters, and if I remember correctly, fudge is one of your favorites."

The fact that he remembered touched something inside of her. Something she'd been trying really hard to ignore.

"It is."

"Care to join me, then?"

"Sure." She stood as Ms. Milly's words replayed in her mind.

True love transcends our pasts, our hurts and our circumstances.

Could she be right?

Jillian shook her head. She had no idea how Gabriel felt about her. Unlike his grandfather, he hadn't expressed his feelings. Even if he had—

But there is one thing you have to do.

Be willing to accept it.

Sadly, Jillian had so many doubts, she wasn't sure she'd ever be able to do that.

"Oh. My. Word." Peering out the side door of the youth barn Saturday morning, Gabriel scanned the line of people stretching from the front door of the building to the parking lot that was overflowing with vehicles while more lined the road in front of the church even before their start time of eight o'clock.

Panic clipping through his veins, he stepped back inside, closing the door as he surveyed the space where colorful lights draped across the rafters, a Christmas tree glowed in the foyer and holiday music filled the air.

"The grandmothers are here."

Gabriel turned as Ricky approached.

"Something wrong?" The youth minister who'd volunteered to pick up Mamaw and Ms. Ida Mae eyed him curiously. "You look like you're about to be sick."

"Have you looked outside?"

"Just came from there. We've got quite a turn-out."

"Or we've bitten off more than we can chew." Gabriel moved to the center of the large space and whistled to get everyone's attention. "People!"

Around thirty kids and adults alike who'd volunteered to help today turned their attention his way.

"We are about to be overwhelmed." He poked a thumb over his shoulder. "There are *hundreds* of people out there."

Stepping away from the grandmas, Jillian hurried toward him with Aggie in tow. "Which is exactly what we were hoping for." Her smile was wide as she scanned the group.

"Huh?" Gabriel stared at her. Obviously she hadn't looked outside.

"Yes, we have a considerable crowd waiting to do some holiday shopping. However, we will not be overwhelmed, thanks to something called *fire codes*. They dictate how many people can be inside a building at one time. So I'm going to let our favorite deputy, Brady James, explain how things are going to work today."

Gabriel and Jillian moved aside while Brady stepped forward amid a round of applause.

Tugging Gabriel toward the outside wall, Jillian turned to face him. "Are you trying to scare everyone off?" she whispered.

"What do you mean?"

"You were in a panic." With Aggie between them, Jillian leaned closer, keeping her voice low.

He inhaled the fruity scent of her shampoo. "No, I wasn't." When his voice cracked, he cleared his throat. "Okay. Maybe a little. But you didn't see all those people out there. How did you know about the capacity thing?"

Her head tilted toward his. "I work in a city building. And all those people are part and parcel of a successful bazaar."

The woman was as smart as she was beautiful. Talk about a dangerous combination. "Have I told you how glad I am you're helping me with this?"

She looked up at him with those blue eyes that never failed to pierce his heart. "Your Christmas-tree surprise more than makes up for it."

"Oh, yeah?" Suddenly, his anxiety was forgotten.

"Yes."

Then Brady's voice penetrated his musings. "Doesn't mean you're not going to be busy, though, so keep your wits about you, don't stress and, above all, be friendly."

Uh-oh. Gabriel had been so engrossed in Jillian, he hadn't heard most of what Brady had said.

"You may be the only example of Jesus some of these people will ever see."

As Brady returned to where he'd been standing before Jillian called him up, Gabriel moved to the spot his friend had vacated. "Brady makes a good point. We are called to love one another. Even those who might be a little—shall we say—*difficult*."

People chuckled.

"Yes, you know what I'm talking about." He

looked at Jillian. “Anything you’d like to add, Jillian?”

She strolled toward him. “Hmm. I find it rather interesting you give me the floor right after referring to difficult people.”

The group laughed once again.

“Just to piggyback on what Brady and Gabriel said,” she began, “less than two weeks ago, we thought all hope was lost and we’d have to cancel the bazaar. But because Gloriana Broussard—” Jillian motioned her way “—was willing to step up and sound the alarm across our entire region, God opened the floodgates that allowed us to be here today. So let’s smile and help others do the same.”

“All right, gang.” Gabriel clasped his hands together. “Let’s bow our heads for a word of prayer.” When he’d finished, he hollered, “Places, everyone.”

While youth and adults alike scattered, he joined the grandmas as they pushed their walkers toward the double doors of the gym, where they planned to greet all who entered.

“You ladies doing okay?”

“Better than you.” Mamaw snickered, as did her friend.

“Yeah, go ahead and rub it in. Even the toughest guys can have moments of weakness.”

The women paused this side of the doorway.

"Don't you worry about us, Gabriel," said Ms. Ida Mae. "We all have our fortes. You do your thing, and we'll do ours."

"Yes, ma'am."

Moments later, the doors opened, and the first group of people entered. Some rushed right in, while others paused to get a feel for things.

Popular items that people were apt to grab multiples of since they were deeply discounted had been marked with signs and labels indicating only one per person. The last thing they wanted was one person scooping them all up and then reselling them. Gabriel hated that he even thought that way, but he knew it was true. Which was why he'd borrowed the idea from popular retailers and their Black Friday sales.

As the morning progressed, Gabriel began to realize just how right Jillian had been about him overreacting. And as they approached noontime without incident, he recognized she'd saved him from embarrassment. Strange how they seemed to have shifted roles. Ever since she'd moved to Hope Crossing, he'd been the one to calm her down, and understandably so. But today it had been just the opposite. It felt kind of good knowing someone had his back.

Later, he found himself watching her as she mingled with shoppers, offering advice and making suggestions. She'd even entertained some of the little ones while their parents shopped.

More and more, the old Jillian was slowly coming out of hiding. And while Gabriel had always been drawn to her, this beautiful butterfly was growing comfortable with her new wings. Leaving him smitten all over again.

Right now, though, he couldn't help noticing she seemed a little pale. Her smile wasn't quite as bright either. And Aggie was sticking to her like glue. Perhaps Jillian was doing too much or was tiring. She'd admitted on their ride to the church before sunup that she'd been too excited to sleep last night. And she'd been running around like a busy bee since they arrived. He'd stopped by the kitchen a few times to partake in the snacks several church members had brought by for the workers. But what about Jillian? The last thing he needed to worry about was her blood sugar dropping.

As she waved goodbye to a little boy and girl she'd been playing with, Gabriel approached. "Tired?"

She waved him off. "I'm fine."

"Have you been to the kitchen for a bite to eat yet?"

"No time. I'm having too much fun."

"Said my six-year-old nephew."

She quirked a brow in that cute little way she had.

"Do I need to remind you that you're eating for two?"

She sighed. "I guess I could stand to grab a quick snack."

"In that case, follow me." He offered his elbow and was pleased when she took hold.

Once they were in the kitchen and out of view of shoppers and workers alike, he pointed to the island. "We have sandwiches and fruit. Some snack mix, granola bars and, naturally, half a dozen holiday treats of one variety or another." He reached into his pocket for some dog treats. "Aggie, I haven't forgotten you."

The poodle wagged her tail as she approached to take one from his hand.

"Ooh, fudge."

"Oh, no you don't." He grabbed a plate and handed it to Jillian. "Not until you've had a sandwich."

Her brow lifted again. "You're being awful bossy."

"That's because I can't focus on the bazaar if I'm worried about you."

Taking hold of the plate, she reached for a ham salad sandwich half. "You don't need to worry about me."

"Look, I'm not trying to be bossy, Jillian. I just happen to care about you." Perhaps too much. "You and your baby."

"In that case..." Pink suffused her cheeks as she took a bite of the sandwich.

"Thank you. Now, do I need to stay here and make sure you eat more than just that sandwich and some fudge, or can I go back out there, confident that you'll make wise choices?"

"I promise I'll be good. Now get back out there before they wonder where we are."

He did just that, and in the nick of time, it seemed, as another flood of customers waited to get inside. Thankfully, it was a beautiful early December day.

Yet as the day progressed, he found himself hoping for some time alone with Jillian this evening. Assuming she wasn't too tired. After all, they'd worked hard and deserved a little celebration. Though, he had no idea what that might look like.

When the last customers had left and the doors were closed at three that afternoon, everyone was as exhilarated as they were exhausted. So while some boxed up the remaining goods, most of which would be donated to a shelter for abused women and children, Gabriel, Jillian and the grandmas tallied up how much they'd made. To their surprise, it was double what they'd hoped for. And when they made the announcement, everyone went wild. Combined with the monetary donations people had given in lieu of items, the youth would have plenty to cover their mission trip and then some.

Gabriel had never seen the kids so excited. Some were even asking if they could do it again next year.

When the teens finally quieted, Ricky said, "This was a group effort, so you all should be proud of yourselves. Though, I have to say, none of this would've been possible without two grandmothers who wanted to help y'all achieve your dream." He pointed to the grandmas, sitting atop their walker seats, looking like they were ready for a nap. "You ladies are an inspiration to us all."

Not long after that, Gabriel and Jillian were on their way to the assisted living to drop off their grandmothers.

"I believe I'm going to sleep good tonight," Ms. Ida Mae said.

"Ain't that the truth," Mamaw responded.

They did look tired. But they were also beaming from a job well done.

When Gabriel finally pulled into his own driveway, he looked Jillian's way. "Could I interest you in a celebratory dinner?"

"What did you have in mind?"

"Frozen pizza or leftover soup. Take your pick."

She grinned. "Wow, you're pulling out all the stops."

"I wish I could, but I'm too exhausted."

"It's a good exhausted, though," she said with a smile.

"So what do you say?"

"My place or yours?"

"How about yours so we can enjoy that beautiful Christmas tree?"

"Let's go, then."

Less than an hour later, they were eating their frozen supreme pizza on the sofa in Jillian's living room, Aggie at their feet, while a Christmas movie played on the television.

When it went to commercial, Jillian set her now-empty plate atop his on the coffee table and drew one leg under her as she twisted to face him. "Thank you for being so perceptive earlier today and encouraging me to eat. You always seem to have my back." Her blue eyes were laser-focused on his.

He reached for her hand, his gaze never leaving hers. "That's because I care about you." His heart kicked into overdrive, his stomach knotting like a teenager on his first date.

As old feelings sprang to life, he mustered a morsel of confidence. He lowered his head just a notch to see what she would do.

She didn't move. Her eyes sparkled. When her lips parted, he leaned closer—

His phone rang, killing the mood.

With a soft chuckle, she leaned away.

Groaning, he dug into his jeans pocket for his phone. "I may have to do bodily harm to whoever this is." His gut tightened when he looked at the screen. "It's Doc's son." He touched the screen, dread slithering up his spine as he placed the phone to his ear. "Hello?"

"Gabriel? Edward Grinnell. I'm afraid I have some bad news."

Gabriel's heart all but stopped.

"My father passed away this evening."

Chapter Eleven

Tuesday was a beautiful, almost perfect day with a brilliant blue sky and temperatures in the low seventies. The kind of day that made you want to be outdoors. Instead, Gabriel was attending a funeral.

At the request of Doc's children, he'd eulogized his friend and mentor and served as a pallbearer. It was one of the first things Edward had asked him when he'd called Gabriel Saturday night. His second query was about the clinic.

"Would you be willing to keep things running for now?"

For now? Funny how those two little words tacked onto an otherwise benign question could evoke such uncertainty. Gabriel had wanted to press Edward. To find out what their intentions were, but it wasn't the time. Not when they were in the midst of planning a funeral.

So Gabriel had promised to keep things status quo at the clinic, all the while wondering for how long. And whether or not the clinic would be his as he and Doc had so often discussed. Had the man mentioned anything to his children? Then again, it was only verbal. They'd never had any formal paperwork.

So until Gabriel heard otherwise, he would continue to carry on the decades of animal care Doc had provided for the community. There were employees counting on him for their livelihood. He'd called each of them before church Sunday morning to let them know of Doc's passing, and that Monday would be a regular workday. However, they would close Tuesday so everyone could attend the funeral.

At the clinic early Monday morning, he'd told the employees they would carry on as usual. More than one had asked if he'd be taking over the clinic. And it had pained him to say he didn't know but assured them that as long as he was there, their jobs were secure.

Now that the funeral was behind them, Gabriel needed to schedule a time to talk with Edward, perhaps his brother, Randall, too, to hopefully learn what their plans were for the clinic. Worst case, Gabriel would purchase it himself. Even though the business had been promised to him.

Now as he sat with Mamaw, Ms. Ida Mae and

Jillian inside the youth barn where the majority of Hope Crossing's population had gathered for the funeral reception, Gabriel watched and awaited that opportunity to ask Doc's sons about such a meeting.

Feeling a hand on his arm, he lifted his gaze to look into Jillian's sweet face. Just the sight of her brightened his mood.

Aggie lay contentedly between them, though he could tell she sensed his grief in the way she often nudged his hand and now rested her head atop his boots.

"Can I get you anything else to eat?" Jillian continued to watch him.

"No, thanks. I'm good."

With a final pat, she retrieved his empty plate from the table and added it to the other three already in her hand before walking away.

He couldn't help wondering what kind of shape he'd be in if it wasn't for her. Edward's phone call Saturday night had dealt Gabriel a blow on many fronts. Yet despite her exhaustion from a long day at the bazaar, Jillian had talked with him late into the night, listening to his stories of working with Doc as a teen and the pride he'd felt when he'd crossed that stage in College Station to receive his doctorate in veterinary medicine knowing his mentor was there to celebrate with him.

So much of his life had revolved around Doc. Making Gabriel feel kind of guilty for the complaining he'd done of late. How could he fault the man for wanting to keep doing what he'd been so passionate about for more than fifty years?

"Gabriel?"

He turned his attention to his grandmother beside him. "Yes, ma'am?"

"Would you be a dear and get Ida Mae and me some dessert, please? With this crowd, I'm afraid it would take us forever."

He scanned the mass of people, some seated, others milling about as multiple conversations filled the large space adorned with Christmas lights. "Of course." He pushed his chair out and stood. "I'll be right back." Then he glanced down at Aggie. "Stay, girl. Jillian will be right back."

Midway to the dessert table, a client stopped him. "Good to see you, Gabriel." The older rancher shook his hand. "It's a shame about Doc, but not unexpected. I reckon you'll be takin' over the animal clinic, huh?"

How Gabriel wished he could say *yes*. But until he knew for certain, he'd keep his comments neutral. "We'll have to wait and see." Then he continued on to the dessert table before the man could ask any more questions.

Until someone else grabbed his arm just as

he was about to snag two slices of chocolate sheet cake.

"Gabriel, that eulogy you gave was so heartfelt," said Mazie Barnhart. "Had me in tears. Some from cryin', some from laughin'."

"Thank you, Ms. Mazie." Hoping to change the subject, he said, "How's ol' Chester doing?" Her donkey was prone to trouble.

"Staying out of my garden, thankfully."

He chuckled at her exasperation. Until he spotted Doc's youngest son, Randall.

Gabriel excused himself and hurried toward him.

Seeing him coming, Doc's secondborn smiled and extended his hand. "Wonderful job on the eulogy, Gabriel. Those stories about our father were just what we'd hoped to hear. You knew him as well as any of us kids."

Gabriel liked to think so. He and Doc had a common interest his children hadn't shared. "Thank you. I had a tough time narrowing down which stories to share. But it's good to have a little comic relief at a funeral."

"Agreed. My father knew how to laugh and have a good time, and your eulogy reflected that."

"I don't know how long you and your siblings plan to be here," said Gabriel, "but I'd like sit down with you and discuss the future of the clinic."

"Absolutely." Randall clamped a hand onto Gabriel's shoulder, as though they were friends. "You've been our father's right-hand man for many a year, and he thought very highly of you."

Not highly enough to follow through on his promise.

The truth of that felt like a sucker punch.

"My brother has your number," Randall continued, "so I'm sure he'll be in touch with you soon."

"Great. Thanks." Returning for the grandmas' cake, Gabriel finally felt a morsel of hope. He'd need to put pen to paper to determine what kind of offer he could make, though.

After grabbing the cake, he was stopped at least two more times. And each person asked about the clinic. Seemed everyone had made the assumption that he would be the heir to Doc's veterinary throne. If only it was true.

As the crowd began to dwindle, Gabriel and Jillian accompanied the grandmas as they paid their respects to Doc's daughters.

While they chatted, Jillian cocked her head and looked up at him. "How are you doing?"

He didn't have a response. If anything, he felt numb. So he simply shrugged.

With Aggie between them, Jillian reached for his hand and gave it a squeeze. "I'm here for you. Just the way you've been for me countless times."

He squeezed back, managing a smile. "I appreciate that."

"And Gabriel..." He heard Doc's eldest daughter drag his name out.

She approached, arms wide. "Daddy thought of you like a son."

Gabriel returned the hug, wishing that had been the case. He knew Doc cared about him, but a son would've had the security of a future at the clinic. "He meant a lot to me, too, Cathy."

Finally, they made their way toward the foyer only to have the grandmas decide they should use the restroom before leaving.

Pausing near the sitting area, Jillian shook her head. "I may as well join them. Perhaps I can hurry them along."

"Do you want me to keep Aggie?"

"Sure."

Taking hold of Aggie's leash, he watched Jillian go, wishing she didn't have to get back to the library. He could use someone to talk to. Not that he hadn't already talked her ear off about his situation. What he needed was to talk to Doc's kids. He could only hope Edward called him as Randall had suggested.

Then, as if he'd spoken him into existence, he spotted Edward talking with another man near the check-in desk across the way.

Gabriel casually inched in their direction, Aggie's leash in one hand, the other in the pocket of his dark-wash jeans, pretending not to notice them, but ready to swoop in should he have the opportunity.

"So what are you going to do about the veterinary clinic?" the other man asked.

"My siblings and I have already been in contact with a group of partners from Houston who would like to expand," said Edward. "Matter of fact, they're so eager to jump on it, they're coming out here tomorrow to see the place."

Gabriel turned away, feeling as though a fist had slammed into his gut. Aggie nudged his hand, but he ignored her. His worst nightmare had come to life. And from the looks of things, he was helpless to stop it.

Jillian had no idea what had changed between the time she went to the restroom and when they left the youth barn with the grandmas, but Gabriel seemed even more disheartened than before. It broke her heart to see him hurting. She had to find out what was going on. So after returning to the library and checking in with her assistant, Jillian took her leave and went to find him.

Since he'd taken the grandmas to the assisted living, Jillian went there first, but when she didn't see his truck in the parking lot, she continued to the house. Not finding him there either, she went on to the clinic. Despite being closed today on account of the funeral, she had a feeling she might find him there.

Her instincts had been right. Even before she pulled into the parking lot, she spotted his truck near a side door.

After parking her own vehicle next to his, she got out and started toward the door with Aggie at her side. The midafternoon air was pleasant, though the gentle breeze had her brushing her hair away from her face.

Approaching the buff brick building, she shifted her attention to the red metal barn and covered pens behind it, a pang filling her heart. She couldn't help thinking that all of this should be Gabriel's. He was as loyal as they came. Something rare in today's dog-eat-dog world. That kind of devotion deserved to be rewarded.

Trying the door to the clinic, she found it unlocked, so she pushed it open, knocking as she entered. "Gabriel?"

Moments later, he appeared in the hallway. His tie and sports coat were gone, and his hair was a mess from having dragged his fingers through it numerous times. "What are you doing here?"

Jillian immediately dropped Aggie's leash, allowing her to do what Aggie did best.

The poodle trotted his way, eager to offer comfort.

"Coming to see you in your time of need. The way you've done for me."

While he stroked Aggie, Jillian caught up to them. And when Gabriel looked at her with those pain-filled eyes, Jillian couldn't help wrapping her arms around him and holding him tight.

His arms came around her while he buried his face against her neck. She had no idea how long they stood there, but it felt good to be able to give back to this man who'd done so much for so many people. Including her.

When he finally released her, she noticed the lines carved into his brow had grown even deeper.

"I'm sorry." He swiped the sleeve of his button-down shirt over his eyes.

How could he say that after helping her through countless breakdowns? "Don't be." She looked around the narrow corridor. "Is there someplace we can sit down?"

"My office." He turned and motioned for her to follow him into a small, square room with off-white walls lined with diplomas and other credentials. He continued past the large wooden desk to the leather swivel chair beyond and dropped into it as though he was carrying the weight of the world.

Eyeing the two rigid lobby-style chairs in front of the desk, she eased into the first one, pleased when Aggie chose to join Gabriel. Even more so when he responded, rubbing the dog's curly coat.

Hands clasped in her lap, she watched the seemingly defeated man before her. "Gabriel, what happened after I left you in the foyer? Because you seemed to have a little more pep in your step prior to that."

His frown deepening, he stared out the window. "When I spoke with Randall, Doc's younger son, he seemed all on board for meeting with me so we could talk about the future of the clinic. Then, while you and the grandmas were gone, I overheard Doc's oldest son, Edward, talking with someone in the foyer. He said they've got a group of partners coming out to visit the clinic tomorrow." Gabriel puffed out an incredulous laugh. "Not only have I lost my friend and my dream, his son lied to my face about it."

"Gabriel, I am so sorry." His desk felt like a chasm between them. She longed to comfort him the way he'd comforted her so many times. If only there was something she could say or do to make it all go away.

Then she recalled the testimony she'd shared with the church.

The last thing she wanted to do was throw platitudes Gabriel's way. She was all too familiar with them. But she couldn't help thinking about Joseph and the things she'd said that day at church.

She would do anything to help this man she cared so deeply about. "I'm not saying this to placate you, Gabriel, because I understand the kind of pain you're feeling right now. I know how it feels to have a dream stolen from you. That sense of loss and betrayal. But I can promise that God has not forgotten you."

Slouched in his chair, one hand atop his flat stomach while the other remained on Aggie, he stared at Jillian. "Coming from anyone else, those words probably would've frustrated me. But coming from you—" he shrugged "—they carry some weight."

He straightened then, seemingly ignoring Aggie. "I suppose I should start contemplating alternatives regarding my future, since it doesn't look like I'll be here much longer."

"What if the group did purchase the clinic and they wanted you to stay on?" She held out a hand toward Aggie.

"I don't know that I could do that, Jillian. For starters, I'm familiar with how those groups work. The first thing they're going to do is come in here and up the cost of everything. You've been in Hope Crossing long enough to know that's going to go over like a lead balloon. There's no way I could stay here knowing folks were being overcharged."

She nodded as Aggie approached, then petted her back. "You have a vet truck. Could you work out of that? Though, it would mean more traveling." Something he wasn't particularly fond of.

Shaking his head, he said, "I'm afraid that would limit my clients to large animals. And you already know how I feel about that."

"You like the variety." She eyed the vintage regulator clock on the wall to her right, continuing to think, desperately searching for some sort of happy medium. "What if you started your own clinic here in town? You're already established, so you'd have a clientele."

"Except there's no place in Hope Crossing that would be move-in ready. I'd either have to build new or remodel an existing space and either of those would take time." He stood from his chair and raked his fingers through his hair again, looking absolutely beat down. "I'm in a Catch-22 if I stay in Hope Crossing."

Her heart sank. Her feelings for Gabriel ran deep. They had before her assault, and after all he'd done for her since she moved here, the way he'd encouraged her, they'd grown even stronger. "Does that mean you're contemplating leaving?" The thought broke her heart.

"I'm sorry, Jillian." He moved toward her, took

her hands and pulled her to her feet. "I don't know what I'm saying. I'm exhausted."

Peering into his bloodshot eyes, she said, "I know you are. Not only do you need to rest, you need time to process things before you make any decisions."

When he slipped his arms around what was left of her waist and pulled her close, she didn't resist.

About that time, the baby kicked.

Gabriel looked down and grinned. "Was that what I think it was?"

Feeling her cheeks heat, she said, "Welcome to my world. I'm kicked multiple times each day."

"She's an active little thing." His smile had her recalling her conversation with Ms. Milly the other night and how Gabriel's grandfather had loved her son as his own.

Jillian was confident Gabriel would do the same thing. But what about her?

True love transcends our pasts, our hurts and our circumstances.

Could Jillian accept that, though? Could she believe someone loved her despite what had happened?

Gabriel brushed a lock of hair away from her face, his fingers caressing her skin and sending a wave of goose bumps down her arm that made her want to believe it was true. "I'm sorry I shot down all of your options. It's just that I've never imagined being anywhere but here." He looked into her eyes. "So I never bothered to contemplate anything else."

Resting her hands against his broad chest, she said, "I'm happy to be your sounding board anytime you want to run ideas past me."

"I wouldn't have it any other way."

They stared at each other for the longest time, and the yearning for what they had once shared welled inside of her.

"May I kiss you, Jillian?"

While a kiss did not equate to love, the way he looked at her made her feel alive again and gave her hope. "I thought you'd never ask."

He smiled, lowering his head, and pressed his lips to hers.

Though this wasn't the first time they'd ever kissed, it was the first time in a long time. And as his arms enveloped her, drawing her even closer, it felt better than she remembered. These past couple of months their friendship had grown so much deeper, making this moment all the sweeter.

Aggie groaned rather loudly, and both Jillian and Gabriel chuckled.

"Way to kill the moment there, Aggster." He winked at Jillian.

She straightened the collar on his shirt. "Are you sure you're going to be okay?"

He nodded and took a step back. "If I'm not, I know who to come to."

"I can stay, if you'd like. I'm in no hurry."

He took her hand in his. "I think I need to be alone to sort some things out."

Taking hold of Aggie's leash with her free hand, she said, "In that case, I'll be praying that God will give you clarity on what you should do."

"Thanks. That makes two of us."

After insisting he get some rest, she walked out of his office with Aggie at her side and continued down the hallway toward the exit, despite longing to stay. Gabriel was grieving not only the loss of his mentor and friend but the dream that had been snatched away from him. His future was uncertain. She knew what that was like.

As she stepped outside, she prayed God would help Gabriel. Encourage him. And, most of all, provide a way for him to remain in Hope Crossing.

Chapter Twelve

Things at the clinic Wednesday were a little more subdued than usual. Doc was gone, and everyone felt his absence.

Still, they pressed on. Gabriel worked double time, trying to cover both his and Doc's schedules. There were surgeries to be done, patients to see. Gabriel had delivered a litter of puppies from Ned Anderson's favorite hunting dog via emergency C-section after the Weimaraner struggled to deliver. Then the Minkes' ferret got loose, and it took a while to catch the nimble critter.

At least it kept him busy, leaving little time to think about how his life was falling apart. Or to dwell on the memory of Jillian's kiss. The trust behind it was something he would never take for granted.

After such an eventful morning, he was ready for a break. Yet as he glanced at his watch and realized it was already noon, he wondered when Edward would come waltzing into the clinic with that group from Houston. He'd said today, but today ran until midnight. Gabriel wouldn't be surprised if they showed up after hours simply to avoid him.

He found it rather interesting that Edward had yet to say anything to him. Doc's son had never acknowledged him the day of the funeral, so he probably had no idea Gabriel was aware of his plan.

Funny. He never would've pegged Doc's eldest for a coward.

As Gabriel tossed and turned last night, it wasn't just his position at the clinic that had him worried but everyone else's, too. The staff was a well-oiled machine. They knew how to anticipate both Doc's and Gabriel's needs. They were good workers, and he'd hate to see them kicked to the curb.

Retreating to his office, he dropped into his chair and roughed a hand over his face. Why hadn't Doc made arrangements instead of allowing things to fall to his children? Had he just put it off for so long that it slipped his mind like so many other things of late?

About the time he was finishing his lunch of sardines and crackers, Gabriel heard voices—multiple voices—echoing from the hallway.

And as he stepped out of his office, he saw half a dozen people, both male and female, milling about while Edward and his brother, Randall, began spouting off the virtues of the clinic.

"The clinic owns all six acres surrounding this building, so there is plenty of room for expansion," said Randall as the potential buyers tried to find a place to stand in the narrow space. Which was probably why Randall was touting the extra acreage right out of the chute.

Crossing his arms over his chest, Gabriel cleared his throat somewhat loudly, wanting to make sure both Edward and Randall knew he was there. Then chuckled when the visitors jerked their heads his way as though they'd been caught red-handed.

He lowered his arms as he moved toward Doc's sons. "Edward. Randall." He nodded to each of them. "What brings you into the clinic today?"

"I thought you called him." Randall scowled at his older brother.

Edward lifted his chin a notch higher. Just enough to look down his nose at Gabriel. "We are merely looking after the best interests of our father's clinic. Our guests represent one of the top veterinary groups in the state of Texas."

"Is that so?" Gabriel eyed the preppy bunch.

"We'd like to show them around the clinic, if you don't mind," said Edward.

Gabriel made a show of checking his watch. "I think the schedule is clear for the next forty-five minutes. After that, you'll have to take your little gathering outside."

One of the male doctors addressed Gabriel. "How long have you worked with Dr. Grinnell?"

It had been so long since Gabriel had heard anyone refer to Doc as *Dr. Grinnell*—if he ever had—that he almost lost his train of thought. "Since I was fourteen years old. For the last eleven years as his partner."

The man continued to study him. "So you're familiar with the area as well as the clientele?"

"Very."

"Dr. Vaughn?" The receptionist peeked around the corner.

"What can I do for you, Ginger?" Eager to escape the vultures Doc's sons had brought in, Gabriel turned to follow her to the check-in desk in the lobby. "Edward, you can go ahead and show them around, if you like," he tossed over his shoulder as he retreated.

Once he'd helped Ginger squeeze in a Chihuahua with an eye injury, he returned to his office to escape Edward's guests. But as he settled into his chair, there was a knock on his door.

Looking that way, he saw the doctor who had called Doc Dr. Grinnell. A tall, skinny fellow who didn't look much younger than Gabriel.

"May I help you?"

The other doctor strolled toward Gabriel's desk. "I didn't get the opportunity to introduce myself. I'm Chas Wilmington." He stretched across the desk to shake Gabriel's hand.

He took hold. "Gabriel Vaughn."

Letting go, the man clutched a tablet against his torso. "Yes, so my colleagues and I were wondering if you would be interested in remaining here at the Hope Crossing Veterinary Clinic. That is, assuming we decide to move forward with the purchase. We think you would be a great asset. The locals know and respect you. That's important to us. It would make the transition to unfamiliar faces go much smoother."

Elbows on the arms of his chair, fingers steepled, Gabriel lifted a brow. "Are you asking me to partner with you?"

"Uh, no." Chas's gaze dropped to his shoes momentarily. "More like be the face of the clinic. You'd still practice here, of course, you…just wouldn't be an owner."

If that wasn't a slap in the face, Gabriel didn't know what was.

As he was narrowing his gaze, his phone buzzed in his pocket. Grateful for the diversion, Gabriel checked the screen. Caleb Kendrick? His buddy from veterinary school.

He faced Chas again. "Yeah, let me think on it

and get back to you." Although he already knew his answer.

Never.

Tapping the screen, he sucked in a breath and swiveled his chair so his back was to the door before setting the phone to his ear. "Caleb? Long time no hear." At least a year or so.

"I know. How you doin', buddy?"

"A little rough at the moment, but nothing life-threatening. How about you? How're the wife and kids?"

"Good. Actually, we have a new baby. She's three months old now."

Gabriel could hear the pride in his friend's voice. Didn't seem that long ago Gabriel was best man at his friend's wedding. Now he had four kids.

Caleb was living the dream. While Gabriel's dreams of a family and his own practice continued to elude him.

"Life is good," said Caleb. "Can't complain."

"I assume you're still in Kerrville?"

"Oh, yeah. I'm not going anywhere. Which leads me to the reason for my call."

Gabriel leaned back in his chair to stare out the window. "Okaaay."

"My partner at the clinic, Dr. Brewster, is planning to retire."

Both Gabriel and Caleb had gone to work for

older veterinarians because they liked the idea of learning from someone who was not only experienced but a little bit old-school. If only Doc hadn't been so set in his ways.

"Which means I'm looking for another partner," Caleb continued. "And you were the first person I thought of."

Gabriel roughed a hand over his face. How many times had he and Caleb discussed opening a clinic together? Back in vet school, it was all they'd talked about as they dreamed of *someday*.

"Wow. I, uh—" Gabriel blew out a breath as he sat up straight. "I'm not free to speak right now, but let's just say the timing of your phone call couldn't be better."

"Does that mean you'll think about it?"

"Yes, I will." Thoughts of Jillian played through his mind. "Though, I have a lot of variables I'll need to weigh out, too."

"I understand. I'm aware that I'm asking you to pack up your life there to join me."

Movement outside the window had Gabriel darting a glance that way. Then he saw Edward, Randall and the group of doctors clustered in the parking lot. Everyone was all smiles. Especially Doc's sons. That could only mean one thing.

Gabriel's blood began to boil. All these years at the clinic, and yet at the first opportunity he was being kicked to the curb. "On second thought,

Caleb, I think I would like to come take a look. Does Saturday work for you?"

"Yeah." Caleb was obviously surprised by Gabriel's sudden change of heart. "Absolutely. I'll text you the address. Just tell me what time to meet you."

"Great. I'll see you Saturday."

Gabriel clutched the phone in his hand long after the call had ended, a wealth of emotions churning inside of him. How interesting that Caleb would call just as that punk doctor was trying to convince Gabriel to stay on here. But it was no coincidence.

Two raps sounded at the door and one of the techs poked her head inside. "The Chihuahua is in room two."

"I'll be right there." Standing from his desk, he saw the bright sunshine filter through the trees outside the window. And Gabriel couldn't help wondering: *God, what are You up to?*

"The baby is measuring right where she should at thirty-four weeks," Jillian's obstetrician said Friday morning. "However, you didn't gain as much weight as I would have preferred." Dr. Mossier's dark gaze remained fixed on Jillian. "You look tired, too. Are you getting enough rest?"

"Sometimes." Jillian petted Aggie, who sat

beside her. "In my defense, this has been an unusual couple of weeks." From the busyness of the bazaar to the grief of Doc's passing and the uncertainty of Gabriel's future, not to mention one incredible kiss. To make matters worse, she hadn't seen him much since then. She'd invited him to join her for dinner almost every night, but he'd declined every time, saying he had a lot on his mind.

After promising her doctor she would pay closer attention to her diet, Jillian scheduled her next appointment for two days after Christmas. And minutes later, she and Aggie were on their way back to the library. Giving her twenty minutes to stew on the fact that while she'd leaned so heavily on Gabriel since moving to Hope Crossing, he wouldn't allow her to be there for him. Instead, he kept putting her off with excuse after excuse.

You could force his hand.

Hmm. Winding through the countryside, she eyed the gray sky.

Instead of inviting Gabriel to dinner, maybe she should take dinner to him. Then insist she stay and join him. And tonight might be a good night to do that. Since the weather had turned cold, she'd started a batch of southwest chicken soup in the slow cooker this morning. There was more than enough for just her.

So, Jillian paid Grandmama a quick visit after work that evening, then went home to shred the chicken breasts that had been stewing in the seasoned broth all day. And as she was returning the meat to the pot, headlights shone in the driveway.

Gabriel was home.

Aggie danced toward the door, glancing over her shoulder at Jillian. Making her wonder if her canine friend had sensed Gabriel's grief. Or, perhaps, she was just hoping he'd throw the ball to her. With it getting dark so early, Jillian had only a short window of time once she got home where she felt comfortable being outside alone.

Crossing to the door, she unlocked it to allow Aggie outside. Then stood there, her cardigan wrapped around her middle as she watched both dog and man.

Without so much as a glance toward Jillian's house, Gabriel patted Aggie then tossed the neon-green ball. While Aggie chased after it, Jillian waited to see if Gabriel would acknowledge her.

He didn't.

Something was bothering him, all right. So if he wouldn't come to her, she'd go to him.

She returned to the counter, unplugged the slow cooker and gave the soup a stir before setting the lid atop the pot. Then she grabbed a fresh bag of tortilla chips from the pantry, along with the package of Christmas cookies she'd picked up from Plowman's and placed them in a reusable grocery sack. After slipping the handles of the bag over one arm, she pulled a couple of potholders from the drawer and gathered up the slow cooker.

Making her way onto the porch, she set the pot down on a chair, made sure she had her key, then closed and locked the door behind her.

"What are you doing?" Gabriel watched her as she descended the steps holding the pot and continued toward his house.

"Bringing you supper." She kept walking, determination propelling each and every step.

"Why?" He was behind her now.

Marching up the steps onto his porch, she turned to face him. "Because I thought you might appreciate some hot soup on this chilly evening."

He remained beside his truck, watching her, but not moving.

"Would you mind getting the door for me, please?"

After tossing the ball again, he joined her on the porch.

He unlocked the door. "Let me take this." He grabbed the pot from her, then waited, allowing her to enter first.

Gabriel's kitchen was much more modern than the one at Grandmama's. With Ms. Milly's approval, he'd gutted it and started from scratch, completing most of the work himself.

Instead of the standard white cabinets that were so popular, he'd gone with a light gray, then added a darker gray subway-tile backsplash that, combined with the dark stain he'd used on the original pine floors, gave the space plenty of warmth without looking too rustic.

She bypassed the dark wood table flanked by four gray fabric chairs to stop alongside the white-and-gray solid surface counter. "I brought some chips to go with the soup, as well as some cookies for dessert." She removed them from the bag.

"Thank you, but you didn't have to do this." He set the pot on the counter beside the other items, looking almost nervous.

"I know. But I wanted to. After all you've done for me, Gabriel, this meal is a drop in the bucket." She sucked in a fortifying breath and took advantage of Aggie's nearness by stroking the soft curls atop her head. "I hope you don't mind if I join you."

The way he hesitated, she could tell he wanted to say he did.

Leaving the pot holders on the counter, he shoved his hands into the pockets of his jeans and turned away. "It's been a rough week."

"I understand. What I don't get is why you

won't let me help you sort things out the way you've done for me countless times. Instead, you've barely talked to me since that day I came by the clinic—"

Her insides tangled as she suddenly put two and two together. "Wait. Is this about that kiss?" She dared to step in front of him, wanting to see the look on his face. "Because if it is, you have no need to worry. I didn't read anything into it."

Rubbing the back of his neck, he let go an exasperated breath. "No. It has nothing to do with the kiss."

"Then what is it, Gabriel? Why are you avoiding me? And don't try to deny it. I know you too well."

His shoulders slumped. He sighed. "Doc's sons came into the clinic Wednesday with their potential buyers."

Curiosity had her narrowing her gaze. "Weren't you expecting them?"

"I knew they'd be by at some point based on what I'd overheard Edward say, but they never contacted me to say when. They just showed up." He dragged his fingers through his hair, looking absolutely miserable. "After learning how long I'd been with Doc, one of the visiting doctors asked me if I'd consider staying on."

"That's good, isn't it? How would that work with so many of you, though?"

"He wasn't asking me to be a part of their group, Jillian. He simply wanted me to hang around to make them look good. To be the *face of the clinic*." He used air quotes. "But I wouldn't be a partner."

Indignation burned in Jillian's gut. "He actually said that?"

"Yep." Gabriel moved around the counter to grab a couple of bowls from the cupboard.

Watching him, she said, "I hope you told them *no*."

"I said I'd think about it."

"How…?"

Across from her now, he held up a hand. "Don't worry. I have no intention of doing that."

Phew. "You had me worried for a second."

He retrieved a ladle from a drawer and set it in front of her. "While they were still touring the place, a buddy of mine from veterinary school called. The vet he works with is retiring. Caleb asked me to be his partner."

Removing the lid from the slow cooker, she picked up the ladle. "That's wonderful, Gabriel. Where is his clinic?" She grabbed one of the bowls.

"In Kerrville."

Her movements stilled. Kerrville was at least three hours away, if she wasn't mistaken.

Willing herself to appear indifferent, she continued to ladle the soup. "It sounds like a wonderful opportunity. What did you tell him?" She passed him the bowl.

"Thank you." He set it on the counter. "At first, I said I'd have to think about it. Then I saw Doc's sons outside, shaking hands with the other doctors as though they'd struck a deal." He sucked in a breath. "And I changed my mind. I told Caleb I'd be out there to visit him tomorrow." He stared at the steaming bowl. "I've been vacillating ever since, though, and I've decided to call him and tell him I've changed my mind."

Dipping the ladle into the mixture of chicken, tomatoes, black beans and corn, she glanced up at him. "Why?"

"Because it's too far away. I'd have to pack up and move my entire life out there. That would put me even farther from Mamaw than my folks are."

"I don't think Ms. Milly would want you to give up something you might really enjoy because of her."

Retrieving two spoons from another drawer, he said, "But what if it's not as great as my buddy made it out to be? What if I don't like it?"

"How are you going to know if you don't see it for yourself?" Resting the ladle on a napkin, she returned the lid to the pot.

Gabriel looked at her from the other side of the counter. "What if I *do* like it?"

“Then, you will win over the pet owners of Kerrville and the surrounding areas.” And while her heart would be breaking, she’d never let on to Gabriel. Somehow, she would go on without him. She’d just miss him like crazy.

Chapter Thirteen

Gabriel departed for Kerrville before the sun rose the next morning. Driving through the darkness, he thought about last night and Jillian. The fact that she'd taken the initiative to come to him—not just yesterday, but the day of Doc's funeral—was yet another indication of how far she'd come in recent weeks.

Talking with her last night had helped him reconcile the turmoil that had been raging inside of him for days. And once he'd determined to go to Kerrville with an open mind, he'd been able to enjoy the rest of the evening with her.

After eating at his place, they'd gone back to her house to watch a Christmas movie. There was something about the glow of the Christmas tree in her living room coupled with a sweet movie and Jillian at his side that put him at ease.

Now as he watched the sunrise in his rearview

mirror, he couldn't help wondering if his dream lay ahead in Kerrville, or if he'd left it behind in Hope Crossing.

Save for college and veterinary school, he'd lived his entire life in Hope Crossing. He knew everyone, and they knew him. A move to Kerrville would mean starting over. He'd be the outsider. An unfamiliar face. His entire life would change.

That hadn't bothered you when you were contemplating a move to Dallas.

But there'd been another driving force behind that. Jillian.

He cared about her. Had envisioned a future with her. Now she was in Hope Crossing. Urging him to go to Kerrville.

He thought about the kiss they'd shared at the clinic. How perfectly she fit in his arms. He may have been messed up that day, but that moment had felt so right.

She'd said she hadn't read anything into it.

She might not have, but he certainly had. That kiss had given him hope. Something his life was sorely lacking right now. Which was why he was so torn. Whether he chose to go to Kerrville or stay in Hope Crossing, there would be a lot of uncertainty.

Still, he knew in his heart it was no coincidence Caleb had called when he did. And like

Jillian had said, he couldn't make an informed decision without visiting the place.

Kerrville was a nice town of about twenty-some thousand that sat along the banks of the Guadalupe River in the Texas hill country and had a lot of shopping and dining options. Definitely more than Hope Crossing. Which wasn't difficult, since Plowman's was their only option.

With the help of the navigation on his truck, Gabriel readily located the clinic on the edge of town, not too far from the river. He pulled into the gravel parking lot just after nine thirty and continued toward the off-white metal building that wasn't much bigger than Doc's clinic, with a stone facade like so many buildings throughout the area.

He brought his truck to a stop alongside another pickup, shifted into Park and took a deep breath. "God, I need Your help. Not my will, but Yours. Make it plain to me where You want me to be. In Jesus's name, Amen."

When he looked up, his old buddy was standing at the now-open front door.

Gabriel turned off the engine and stepped out into the cool morning air as Caleb approached. "Hey, man."

The two shook hands before reeling each other in for a brotherly hug.

"I'm glad you're here." Caleb smiled behind a well-groomed beard.

"You're looking a little furrier than the last time I saw you." Gabriel fingered his own stubbled chin. "Finally outgrew that peach-fuzz phase, I see." Truth be known, the other guys were just jealous that Caleb didn't have to shave as often as they did.

"Hey, now. You'd better watch it, Vaughn." His longtime friend shot him a warning look before an expectant smile claimed his face. "Come on, I can't wait to show you around." Turning, Caleb opened the door and headed into the building.

Gabriel followed his friend into a reception area that felt a lot homier than the sterile one at Doc's clinic. Many a time, Gabriel had suggested they paint the walls something besides white and swap the utilitarian metal chairs for more modern ones in an effort to make the space more inviting. But the man always balked, claiming it was a waste of money.

After going over their check-in and appointment system with Gabriel, Caleb showed him the four exam rooms. Yet while they were pretty standard, the surgical suite was state-of-the-art.

"This is incredible." Gabriel wandered the space, scrutinizing every detail. "You use gas anesthesia?"

"For a couple of years now," said Caleb. "It's made a lot of difference in the animals' recovery."

Which was precisely why Gabriel had been trying to talk Doc into it. At least Caleb's partner wasn't afraid to try something new.

Continuing their tour, Gabriel found himself envious of how organized their pharmacy was. That would translate to more efficiency, especially when it came to reordering.

When they'd covered everything inside, they continued outside for an overview of the covered pens that were similar to what Doc had in Hope Crossing, but the Temple Grandin handling system in the barn was another item that had been on Gabriel's wish list for years. The curved chutes were more efficient for treating cattle, causing the animals less stress.

Gabriel's heart raced with anticipation. This place had so many of the things he'd either suggested they do in Hope Crossing or put on his wish list for when the clinic became his.

"So what do you think?" Caleb regarded him as they returned to the front of the building.

Dragging a hand through his hair, Gabriel said, "I'm a bit envious. You've got some things I've only dreamed of having."

"We try to keep up with all the latest technology. So long as it works for us." Caleb paused.

"Why don't you let me take you to lunch, and we can discuss things further over some barbecue?"

Gabriel rubbed his long-empty belly. "Now you're speakin' my language."

Over a couple of sliced-beef sandwiches a short time later, Gabriel explained the events of the past week to his friend sitting on the opposite side of the booth while Christmas music echoed throughout the rustic restaurant.

"In all honestly, I was hoping I wouldn't like your clinic. But I do. *A lot.*" Gabriel let go a sigh. "Doc was pretty old-school, which, as we both know, has its merits. However, he had an aversion to technology or anything newfangled, as he put it." He grabbed another potato chip. "I always figured I'd just make the changes after he passed the clinic to me. But he never did that. Now he's gone, the clinic belongs to his kids and they're planning to sell it to one of those group practices."

"Ouch. So much for loyalty."

"I know, right?" Gabriel popped the chip into his mouth.

Caleb reached for his soda. "Sounds like the timing of my phone call was perfect, then." He took a sip.

Wiping his hands on a napkin, Gabriel said, "I thought so, too. However, there are some extenuating circumstances on my end."

"Such as?"

"My grandmother. She lives in an assisted living in Hope Crossing, and I'm the only family member who still lives there, so I look out for her." He paused, eyeing the tinsel-laden Christmas tree in the corner. "Also…there's a woman I have feelings for."

Caleb's brow lifted. "What kind of feelings?"

Rubbing his hands over his jeans, Gabriel struggled to come up with an explanation. "It's complicated."

His friend shook his head. "Man, I do not envy you. You're in a tough spot. Sounds like you've got a lot of praying and soul-searching to do."

"Indeed I do. How soon do you need a decision?"

Caleb shrugged. "A month?"

"That shouldn't be a problem."

And on the long drive back to Hope Crossing, Gabriel couldn't help wondering if God was forcing him out of his comfort zone. Encouraging him to step out in faith the way Jillian had. But how was he supposed to choose between becoming a partner in the clinic of his dreams and staying near the two people he cared about the most?

Jillian didn't want to entertain notions of how Gabriel's visit to the clinic in Kerrville was going, so she'd made sure she stayed busy all day. Thankfully, today was the Children's Story Hour at the library, and since it was December, she and Alli had made a party out of it with some easy crafts for the kids, along with a few snacks like those cute pretzel reindeer.

Then, after checking in with Grandmama, she stopped by Plowman's to pick up more butter and eggs so she could do some baking. She'd made ten mini loaves of cranberry nut bread, followed by ten more of pumpkin bread that she planned to give as gifts to the residents and staff at the senior-living community.

While the bread cooled, she made some pecan tassies to take to the fellowship lunch they were having after church tomorrow, followed by a batch of chocolate crinkles. They were Grandmama's favorite. Gabriel's, too, though Jillian wasn't about to admit she made them just for him. He might think she was trying to guilt him into staying.

All afternoon she'd tried to imagine what her life would be like without him living next door. He was probably the closest friend she'd ever had. And that friendship had only grown since she'd moved here. Maybe even blossoming into something more again.

But that would change if Gabriel moved to Kerrville. Sure, they'd probably promise to stay in touch, but then they'd go on with their lives and slowly grow apart.

That didn't happen when you were in Dallas.

No, it hadn't. Because she came down here as often as she could. But then, it was only her. Piling into the car after work on a Friday and driving for hours wouldn't be so easy with an infant in tow.

Maybe Gabriel would come here.

She'd rather not get her hopes up.

With the delightful aromas filling Grandma-ma's kitchen, Jillian slid the cookie sheets into the oven, noting it was almost five o'clock. A glance toward the window revealed Gabriel had yet to return. Perhaps the rain that had moved in this afternoon had slowed him down. But then, he and his friend probably had a lot to discuss. Especially if Gabriel had decided to accept the partnership.

Trying to ignore the pang in her heart, she put the bowl in the sink and added a squirt of deter-gent before filling it with water. Normally, she would've licked the bowl, but since being preg-nant, she'd avoided doing so because of the raw eggs.

She placed a hand on her abdomen. "I guess that won't be the last sacrifice I make for you." But she didn't mind. It would be worth it when she held her little girl. Though right now, it felt as if there was a soccer match going on inside of her. "Take it easy, little one."

After washing the utensils, she set them on the drying mat while she washed and rinsed the mixing bowl. She was reaching for the towel on the counter when she saw Gabriel's truck pull into the drive. The rain was visible in his headlights and coming down at a pretty good rate.

Drying the bowl, she watched as he got out of his truck and hurried toward her house. At least he wasn't avoiding her anymore. Though, she wasn't sure she wanted to hear if he'd made a decision.

By the time he ducked onto her porch, she'd left the bowl on the counter and moved to unlock the door with Aggie at her side. Her canine friend had been unusually clingy today, so perhaps she was missing Gabriel. "Who is it, girl?"

The dog's docked tail wagged back and forth in anticipation.

"Come on in," Jillian said as she swung the door wide.

"Man." He shivered. "It's really coming down out there."

Spotting the plastic bag in his hand with the logo of a beaver on the side, Jillian froze. "Is that what I think it is?"

"I remembered your affinity for salted caramel beaver nuggets—" he handed her the bag "—so when I saw a Buc-ee's I had to pull in and get you some."

"Thank you!" The anticipation nearly overwhelmed her as she removed the bag of delicious salty sweetness from the larger bag. She wasted no time tearing it open, then grabbed a handful of nuggets and popped one in her mouth. "Mmm..." She closed her eyes. "Just as yummy as ever." Still holding the bag in one hand, she offered it to him. "Care for some?"

He held up a hand. "No. Not my thing. However, it smells incredible in here." He strolled toward the counter.

"The weather made this a perfect day for baking."

He perused the bread loaves and the tassies. "I smell chocolate."

She whisked past him to the oven and set the nuggets on the counter. "Chocolate crinkles will be ready shortly."

He lifted a brow. "My favorite."

"Grandmama's, too." She pressed her hands against the ache in the small of her back and stretched. "I'll tell you what, this little one sure has been active today. Feels like she's doing gymnastics." Thinking of all the treats she'd had today, she said, "Perhaps I've had too much sugar and it's gotten to her."

Gabriel eyed the counter again. "From the looks of things, you've been on your feet all day."

The timer went off for the cookies.

As she pulled the pans from the oven, Gabriel continued. "Once you get those squared away, let's sit down in the living room so you can put your feet up."

"And you can tell me how things went in Kerrville."

After moving the cookies to a cooling rack and adding a few to a plate for Gabriel, she continued through the dining room to find him pacing in front of the Christmas tree. He looked nervous. And that made her nervous.

Had he decided to accept the offer?

"I brought you some cookies."

"Great. Thanks." To her surprise, he didn't eat one. He simply set the plate aside.

She eased onto the couch and perched her feet on the edge of the coffee table as Aggie hopped up next to her and laid her head in Jillian's lap. "How was your visit with Caleb?"

"It went well. The clinic is amazing. Pretty much everything I've ever dreamed of for Doc's place but he wasn't willing to do. They even have the Temple Grandin chutes for working with cattle." The excitement in his voice was hard to miss.

"I remember you mentioning that before. You

wanted to add them to the barn at the clinic." But Doc had dismissed it.

"That's right." He dropped beside her on the sofa. "On the drive home, I had a lot of time to think. Not just about Caleb's clinic but about my options here."

She thought they'd gone over them that day at the clinic.

Twisting to face her, he reached for her hand. "For now, I'm going to stay in Hope Crossing and work as a large-animal vet."

That didn't make any sense. Not after he'd been so impressed with the place in Kerrville. "But that's not what you want to do." He'd listed the reasons the other day.

"It's okay. I'll adjust."

Why would he want to adjust when he could be living out his dream? "I don't understand. Why would you do that, Gabriel?"

He caressed her knuckles with his thumb. "Because I need to be here."

"Why?"

"Mamaw needs me." He moved his hand to cup Jillian's cheek. "And so do you."

Those four little words broke Jillian's heart into a million tiny pieces.

This was her fault. She'd leaned on him so heavily since coming to Hope Crossing that he now believed she couldn't get along without him.

And his personality was that of a caretaker. The guy who stepped in to fix whatever was wrong.

Though she would miss him terribly, she would not allow Gabriel to give up his dream because of her. He needed to be free to do what he loved most. To live out his dream.

What was it Grandmama used to say whenever she lost something or had a broken heart? *If you love something, set it free. If it's meant to be...*

Jillian couldn't afford to dwell on that last part. She had to let Gabriel go.

Willing herself to remain strong, she removed his hand and looked into his eyes. "No, Gabriel, I don't need you. I did. And you've been a great friend. You've helped me in more ways than I could have imagined. You gave me Aggie, and she's changed my life. Because of her, I'm much stronger. Strong enough to stand on my own."

He looked at her curiously. "Are you saying you want me to take the job?"

"Yes. It's time for you to stop worrying about everyone else and focus on what *you* want for a change. We'll be okay. I'll take care of your grandmother. You need to live out *your* dream, not give it up for someone else. You have to follow your heart."

Even if it broke hers.

Chapter Fourteen

Gabriel flopped over on his bed, his bedside clock mocking him with blue numbers that read 1:36. After Jillian had insisted he take the partnership with Caleb, there'd been nothing more to say. So he'd tucked his tail between his legs and returned to his house, where he'd been sulking ever since. Because as much as he hated to admit it, she was right.

All these years, he'd clung to Doc's promise and never once contemplated leaving. Until he and Jillian started seeing each other more than a year ago and his feelings began to grow. Gabriel had been ready to move to Dallas so he could be closer to Jillian.

And then that dream fell apart. Now, just when it seemed he and Jillian had been given a second chance, his dream of owning the clinic here was snatched away and he'd been offered the opportunity of a lifetime. Except it was three hours away.

Gabriel stared into the darkness. “God, what am I supposed to do with this? The desires of my heart—both of them—are right there in front of me. Yet if I choose one, I’ll lose the other.”

I don’t need you.

Jillian’s words stung. And seemed to contradict the kiss they’d shared. But ever since she had stood before the church to give her testimony, she’d been growing stronger and more independent.

If he accepted Caleb’s offer, Gabriel would have everything he’d ever dreamed of. Except Jillian, the only woman who’d ever captured his heart.

But she was right. She didn’t need him anymore.

Another glance at the clock: 1:38.

He groaned. If he could just go to sleep, he might be able to escape the torment for a little while.

When he’d pulled in the driveway, he was certain he’d made the right decision. The entire drive back he’d prayed that God would grant him direction. Just when he thought he’d gotten a grasp on things, Jillian upended everything. Why?

Because she wants you to be happy.

Didn’t she realize being with her made him happy? Just the way it had this past spring. He’d spent five painful months without her. Now that they'd found their way back not only to where they'd once been but to something deeper, he didn't want to be without her again.

A strange sound caught his attention.

Gabriel stilled and listened more closely.

There it was again.

Then he heard a bark.

Aggie? She didn't bark unless there was a reason.

He tossed the covers aside and hurried into the kitchen while the poodle continued to bark. Something wasn't right.

Jerking open the door, he saw Aggie darting back and forth between his and Jillian's houses. Then he noticed the light on in Jillian's kitchen. Just like that first night she'd arrived.

Aggie barked again. This time right in front of him.

"All right, girl. I'm right behind you."

The dog bolted across the two driveways and bounded onto the porch with Gabriel trailing. The cold night air nipped at his ears and his bare feet. At least it wasn't raining anymore.

He leaped onto the porch and opened the screen door. Through the split in the curtain, he could see Jillian standing near the counter, hands pressed against the small of her back, a grimace on her face.

He knocked. "Jillian, it's me."

"Come in."

When he opened the door, Aggie rushed past him, but he was on her heels.

The aromas of countless baked goods still hung in the air.

"What's going on, Jillian?" Though he was freaking out inside, he used his doctor voice, praying he sounded calm.

"My water broke. Contractions are six minutes apart."

Her baby wasn't due for another six weeks.

He was certain his heart stopped beating before he regained his wits.

She met his gaze then. "I called my doctor. The hospital in Brenham doesn't have a NICU so she wants me to go to College Station. I need to call an ambulance."

"No, you don't. I'll take you." Maybe he could get Brady to give them a police escort.

Still watching her, he said, "How long has this been going on?"

"My lower back has been aching on and off all day. I thought it was because I was on my feet so much. The contractions woke me up about an hour ago. And when I got out of bed, my water broke—" Her wince told him she was having another contraction.

Moving beside her, he wrapped one arm around her and held her hand with the other.

"Deep breaths. In through your nose." He did it right along with her. "Exhale slowly through your mouth." Again, he led by example. "In… Out…"

Slowly, her body began to relax. She looked up at him. "Thank you."

"You're welcome. Now, let's get you to the hospital." Because while he was confident he could deliver a human baby, this one was way too early. And with an hour's drive to College Station… "Do you have a bag ready?"

She shook her head. "I didn't think I'd need it this soon."

"Can you put one together while I go grab some shoes or would you like me to do it?"

She sent him a nervous smile. "I can do it."

"In that case, I'll be right back."

Since it was the middle of the night, he decided against contacting Brady. If Gabriel got pulled over, he'd simply ask that officer for an escort.

A short time later, they were on the road. Aggie had seemed somewhat confused that they were leaving her behind. Since she was so attuned to Jillian, she would've sensed something was wrong, so she probably wasn't too pleased with the decision, but Gabriel didn't have much choice. Even though service dogs were allowed in hospitals, that didn't apply to sterile environments, so it was best to leave her at Jillian's, and Gabriel could bring her later.

His only concern now was that the little one would decide to make an appearance before they were safely inside the hospital. He'd grabbed some towels and a few supplies from his vet truck, just in case, but he prayed it didn't come to that.

While he drove, Jillian texted her parents to let them know she was in labor. "I don't expect they'll see my message until morning since they both turn off their phones at night, but at least I can say I told them."

"You might be too busy to talk by then. What about your grandmother?"

"I texted her, too. She's not a fan of texting, though, so if she can't get a hold of me, she'll probably call you."

He smiled. "Since she's an early riser, I'll try to give her a call once the sun comes up."

She looked down at her clasped hands. "I'm scared, Gabriel. She's not due for six weeks."

He couldn't help reaching for Jillian. If he weren't driving, he'd take her in his arms. Yet while he wanted to promise her everything would be all right, there were never any guarantees when it came to babies, even if they were full-term.

"First of all, she's not *that* early. Yes, she might have to stay in the hospital a little longer while she learns to breathe and regulate her body temperature and gains a little weight, but she'll have excellent care. This hospital has one of the top NICUs in the region." He squeezed her hand. "The best thing we can do is pray. Like you said, God's got a plan."

"Thank you, Gabriel." Her breath hitched as another contraction hit her. "For everything."

Jillian's doctor had called ahead, so the hospital had a labor-and-delivery room waiting when they arrived. While the nurses got Jillian settled, Gabriel grabbed a cup of coffee and hung out in the waiting room, where paper snowflakes dangled from the ceiling. Lights glowing on the Christmas tree in the corner brightened the otherwise ordinary space.

He stood at the window, looking out into the darkness, praying for a safe delivery and healthy baby.

"Gabriel Vaughn?"

He turned at his name.

The nurse in colorful scrubs said, "Jillian is asking for you."

Those five words had him standing a little taller. Jillian had asked for him. So what if he was the only person in the hospital she knew? She'd asked for him. Wanted him by her side. And there was no place he'd rather be. Whether it was three thirty in the morning or three thirty in the afternoon.

Yet she wanted him to leave Hope Crossing and accept the partnership in Kerrville.

He wasn't going to think about that now. Jillian needed him. And he would be there for her.

Walking into the labor-and-delivery suite, he wasn't sure he'd ever seen anything more beautiful. Her auburn hair splayed over the white pillowcase and her smile took his breath away. Despite the pain she'd been enduring for hours, she was glowing.

And he was smitten all over again.

Over the next hours, Jillian's pain intensified. She'd refused the epidural her doctor offered, claiming this might be the only baby she'd ever have, so she wanted the full experience.

As dawn approached he knew he should contact Ms. Ida Mae. But he couldn't bring himself to break away from Jillian. He didn't care how hard she squeezed his hand. That discomfort paled in comparison to the pain she was experiencing. Though he had to admit, she had a doozy of a grip. His fingertips had turned blue a couple of times.

Now, as they prepared Jillian for delivery, it was time for him to leave.

It was, by far, the hardest thing he'd ever had to do. He didn't want to leave her side. On his drive back from Kerrville, he'd realized just how much he cared for this amazingly strong woman.

She didn't deserve to be left alone with a bunch of strangers while she went through one of the most physically challenging things of her life. He wanted to stay and cheer her across the finish line. But he couldn't.

With their hands fisted together, he kissed her knuckles. "You can do this, Jillian. With or without me. You're strong. And that little girl of yours is eager to meet you. So I'll see you on the other side."

Her face wet with sweat, she panted. "Promise?"

Promise? He'd give her the world. "With all my heart."

He retreated to the empty waiting room and prayed for Jillian and her baby. Then he paced and prayed some more before grabbing another cup of coffee.

Staring out the window as the first shafts of light appeared on the horizon, he bowed his head. *Lord, I can't say that Jillian's baby is too early because everything happens in Your good and perfect timing. But I pray that, despite being so early, Jillian's little girl would be as perfect as she would've been had she gone full-term. That she would be healthy and not have any medical issues. I ask this in the holy name of Jesus, Amen.*

Lifting his head, he decided it was time to call Ms. Ida Mae and let her know what was going on. That is, unless Jillian had beat him to it. Then again, she was a little busy.

Jillian's grandmother answered on the second ring. "Gabriel? How's Jillian? Has she had the baby yet?"

He couldn't help chuckling. It wasn't like Ida Mae to get so riled up. "No baby yet, but it should be anytime. I'm in the waiting room now. Hopefully, I'll have news soon."

"The baby's so early, though."

"Which is why the doctor had Jillian come to College Station. They have a level-three neonatal intensive care unit, so she'll be in good hands."

"I pray so. And I'm gonna go grab Milly and set her to praying, too. We want this baby healthy and full of life."

"Either Jillian or I will contact you as soon as possible." He was tucking his phone away when he heard someone call his name.

Turning, he saw a woman dressed in scrubs, her hair tucked beneath a surgical cap.

She started toward him. "I'm Dr. Mossier, Jillian's doctor." She held out her hand.

He took hold of it. "How is she?"

"Tired but thrilled to be holding her baby. She's a remarkable woman." The doctor smiled.

Aware that Jillian had shared her story with the doctor, he said, "Yes, she is." He hesitated. "How is the baby?"

"So far, so good. The nurses will be monitoring...*it* closely."

He grinned. "*It* was supposed to be a girl. Did that change?"

Pink colored the woman's cheeks. "No. I didn't know if she'd told you or not. I don't like to ruin anyone's surprise."

"I understand. When can I see her?"

"You're welcome to join her now."

A swell of emotions tangled inside of him. Pride. Apprehension. Excitement. "Okay."

When he reached Jillian's room, he paused to take a deep breath. Then he rapped his knuckles against the door before opening it just a crack. "Am I okay to come in?"

"You're more than okay." A nurse opened the door wide.

Stepping inside, he saw Jillian holding the tiniest baby he'd ever seen. Human, anyway. And it took his breath away.

He approached slowly. "She's so little." Beside the bed now, he leaned to press a kiss to Jillian's forehead. "How are you?" As if her smile didn't say it all.

"Tired. But incredibly happy."

He eyed the sweet child in her arms. "She's beautiful, Jillian."

"Look at this." She pulled the baby's cap back just enough for him see the red hair.

A thrill trickled through him. "She's her mama's girl."

After adjusting the cap, she looked up at him again. "I've picked out a name."

"That was quick. I thought you were undecided."

"That was when I was expecting a February baby. But since she was so eager to celebrate her first Christmas, I've decided to name her Noel."

He felt his smile grow wider. "I like that." He turned his attention to the baby. "What do you think, Noel? Do you like it?"

"Would you like to hold her?"

A lump formed in his throat. "If that's okay." He reached for the tiny bundle and carefully nestled her in the crook of his arm. And when she looked up at him with those blue eyes, his heart swelled with more love than he ever imagined a person could feel. Was this how his grandfather had felt when he'd held Gabriel's father for the first time?

And as he continued to stare at little Noel, he knew leaving her and her mother would be the hardest thing he'd ever had to do.

Once Jillian's parents arrived at the hospital, armed with more flowers and balloons than a New Year's Day parade, Gabriel returned to

Hope Crossing to free Aggie, share photos with the grandmas and get some much-needed rest.

And he'd only seen Jillian once since. When he'd returned Aggie last Thursday, the day Jillian and Noel came home from the hospital. He hadn't dared to hang around, though. It would've only made him long for more, and Jillian had made her feelings clear.

Now as he waited for Doc's attorney to show up at the clinic late the following Monday, Gabriel was feeling more than a little defeated. The man had left numerous messages last week, asking to meet with Gabriel, but he'd ignored them until this morning. No point in putting off the inevitable.

He shook his head. Doc's kids must be eager to close the deal with the buyers. Why else would Doc's lawyer offer to come to Gabriel?

He supposed it was time to go ahead and accept Caleb's offer. Not that Gabriel was all that excited about it anymore. Not when it meant leaving Jillian.

Right at five thirty, Gabriel greeted the attorney, who looked to be in his early fifties. "Mr. Longmire?"

The man smiled as he stepped onto the porch. "Yes. You must be Dr. Vaughn." He extended his hand.

Gabriel took hold. "That I am." He stepped

aside, allowing the man to enter. "I assume this has to do with Doc's kids wanting to sell the clinic."

The man hesitated. "In part." He held out an envelope. "Doc asked me to give this to you after his passing."

Gabriel eyed the white envelope. The ones they used here at the clinic. Taking hold of it, he retrieved the pocketknife from his jeans. Moments later, he unfurled the letterhead and read.

Dear Gabriel. I remember when you came to me as a boy, asking if you could work for me. Do you remember what you said when I asked you why?

Because he wanted to work with animals.

Because you wanted to work with animals. And you never lost that passion. You are one of the best veterinarians I have ever had the pleasure to know. That includes myself. You're full of ideas that, sadly, I prevented you from implementing or exploring. Now you are free to do whatever you please. Despite what my children might be anticipating, I'm giving the clinic and the land around it to you because I know you will not only take good care of it but grow it into something more than I ever imagined. The people of Hope Crossing need you, Gabriel. And I have no doubt you'll take care of them and their animals for years to come.

Gabriel wiped at the tears that had blurred his vision. Cleared his throat. "Is this true? He gave me the clinic?"

"Yes. Doc added a codicil to his will last year."

"But his kids were planning to sell. They brought some folks out here for a tour."

"They mistakenly assumed the clinic was theirs to sell." The man clasped his hands. "They seemed rather disappointed when I informed them only the owner could do that, and they were not the owners."

Gabriel grimaced.

"Don't feel too bad for them. Their father had plenty of land and a couple of other properties with which they can do whatever they wish." The attorney paused. "The will still has to go through probate, but you are free to continue running the business. That is, assuming you want it."

"Are you kidding? I couldn't have asked for better news." He wouldn't have to move. He could stay in Hope Crossing. And do whatever he wanted with the clinic.

Mr. Longmire held out his hand. "Merry Christmas, Dr. Vaughn."

Gabriel gripped the man's hand. "Merry Christmas, indeed."

He could hardly wait to tell Mamaw.

And Jillian. But he hadn't seen her in days. Would she even want to talk to him?

As he aimed his truck toward the assisted living, he felt something stir inside of him. Something he hadn't felt since returning from Kerrville. Hope.

Like Joseph when he was in prison, Gabriel felt as though he'd been forgotten. But God had restored him.

Thank You, Lord!

As he sat with Mamaw in her room a short time later, she said, "That is wonderful news." She clasped her hands together. "I cannot tell you how happy that makes me, Gabriel."

"That makes two of us."

"Have you told Jillian?"

Leaning back, he gripped the arms of the easy chair. "What's the point? She doesn't need me, remember?"

His grandmother frowned. "You know, Gabriel, you're not the only one who knows how to love sacrificially."

He glanced across the small table separating them. "I'm not sure what you're getting at. I didn't say anything about love."

A smile lit her brown eyes. "You didn't have

to. I know you. And what you feel for Jillian isn't something new. It's been simmering for a long time. That's why you were willing to sacrifice your dream job to be with her. But she cares too much for you to let you do it." Mamaw skimmed her silver hair behind one ear. "Gabriel, I've been in Jillian's shoes. Feeling unworthy of love, even when it was staring me right in the face."

"What changed your mind?"

"A man who recognized my fears and loved me in spite of them." She reached across the table to take hold of his hand. "Don't give up on Jillian, Gabriel."

A knock at the door had them both looking that way.

"Can I come in, Milly?"

"Of course, Ida Mae."

Gabriel hurried to open the door, allowing Jillian's grandmother to push her walker into the room, looking somewhat disheartened.

"Gabriel." Her sad eyes widened. "I didn't know you were here."

"How are you doing, Ms. Ida Mae?"

"Oh, I'm all right." She parked her walker in front of Mamaw and sat down on it. "Wish I could say the same for Jilly."

His chest grew tight. "Is something wrong with her?"

"Nothing most new mothers haven't experienced. Now that Cindy's gone back to Dallas, though, Jilly's feeling overwhelmed. Evidently Noel didn't sleep much last night."

"I remember those days," said Mamaw.

Jillian's grandmother sighed. "I just wish I could be there to help her."

Gabriel thought of the night Jillian went into labor. She'd been about to call an ambulance. But he'd wanted to help her. And he wanted to help her now. Even if it meant putting his heart on the line. Only this time he'd be in double trouble. Because not only had Jillian stolen his heart, her little girl had him wrapped around her tiny little finger from the first time he saw her.

He couldn't turn his back on them.

"I'll check on her."

Ms. Ida Mae looked as though a weight had been lifted. "Thank you, Gabriel."

"I'll call and let you know how they're doing."

When Jillian opened the door to him a short time later, dressed in sweatpants and a baggy shirt, holding a fussy Noel, and looking as though she'd been crying herself, he was ready to roll up his sleeves and do whatever he could to help her.

"May I come in?"

After greeting Aggie, he turned his attention to Jillian. "Is she hungry?" He pointed to Noel.

Jillian shook her head, her messy bun wobbling. "She ate thirty minutes ago. And she has a clean diaper."

"In that case, why don't you let me take her while you relax on the couch?"

"Gabriel, I can't—"

"Yes, you can. If you don't take care of yourself, how do you expect to take care of Noel?" He held out his hands. "Now, please?"

Finally, she passed him the swaddled babe.

"I think she's gained an ounce or two." He followed Jillian into the living room where the Christmas tree glowed in front of the window, making a mental note to check that it had enough water.

His chest puffed ever so slightly as Noel quieted.

Easing onto the sofa, Jillian sent him an annoyed look. "Show-off." Aggie hopped beside her, and Jillian's hand automatically went to her. Out of habit or anxiety?

"What can I say?" Gabriel stared at the tiny bundle. "She likes me." If only he could be as certain about her mother as Mamaw was.

Swaying Noel ever so slightly, he caught Jillian's gaze. "Doc's attorney paid me a visit today."

Jillian winced. "About?"

"Would you believe Doc left the clinic to me after all?"

Her mouth dropped open. "No. Did he really?"

"He sure did. Even left me a letter." He fished it out of his jacket pocket and handed it to her.

Tears fell as she read. "Gabriel, this is so sweet." She sniffed, meeting his gaze. "I'm so happy for you. It's what you've always wanted."

That's what he used to think. Yet while it gave him a measure of comfort, there was something he wanted even more. Something that still eluded him.

"It means you're stuck with me as your neighbor, though."

"More like *you're* stuck with *me*." She scratched Aggie's curls.

"It's a sacrifice I'm willing to make." His stomach growled. "Have you had supper yet?"

"No." She pulled a throw over her. "Someone from church dropped off some baked potato soup, though. It's on the stove if you'd like some."

"Sounds delicious." He looked at Noel. "What do you think? Should we get some soup?"

Jillian's daughter looked as though she was hanging on his every word.

Glancing at Jillian, he said, "We'll be right back."

In the kitchen, he worked one-handed, locating a couple of soup mugs and ladling soup into each. After adding spoons, he grabbed a napkin along with one of the mugs and returned to the living room to find Jillian asleep.

Doing an about-face, he returned to the kitchen and sat down at the table. "Looks like you wore your mama out, Noel." He stirred the steaming soup with his free hand. "You know, you really should cut her some slack. This whole mom thing is new to her."

He took a bite, savoring the notes of cheese and bacon. And as he looked around, he realized how much he'd missed being here with Jillian. Her smile. Their playful banter. The cute little way she scrunched her nose.

Mamaw was right. He was in love with Jillian.

Noel yawned.

"Looks like your mama's not the only one who's tired."

As Noel drifted off to sleep, Gabriel finished his soup, thinking about how Jillian had shut him out after her assault. What if he'd gone to Dallas and fought for her—for them—instead of wallowing in self-pity? What they'd had was special. Yet he'd made no attempt to save it.

Was he willing to walk away from a second chance?

Jillian had been right when she said she didn't need him. She'd come a long way and was stronger now.

Thinking about how close they'd become since

she moved to Hope Crossing, despite their ups and downs, had him wondering if, perhaps, they could make this work. That, maybe, she could love him.

Jillian was worth fighting for. And thanks to Doc, Gabriel wasn't going anywhere.

Chapter Fifteen

Jillian could hardly believe Christmas was only three days away. Folding another of Noel's sleepers at the kitchen table Thursday, she took a deep breath. She hadn't felt this well rested since Noel arrived. And it was all because of Gabriel.

Since Monday, he'd come by early each morning to see if she needed any help and spend some time with Noel before heading to the clinic. In the evenings, he did the same, only staying longer.

Gabriel was never afraid to lend a hand, and he'd been a huge comfort to her. But were his actions out of friendship or something more?

The thought drove her nuts. Now she had to know. She couldn't stand it any longer. She had to tell Gabriel she loved him. What happened after that? Well, only the Lord knew for sure.

Twelve days ago, Jillian had been prepared to

let Gabriel go. Now the clinic was his and he'd be staying in Hope Crossing. She was as thrilled as she was terrified. Because now she had to admit her true feelings for him. He cared about her and Noel, of that she was certain. But to what extent was a giant question mark.

Where did they go from here?

That was why she had to let him know how she felt.

The timer went off.

She paused her folding to cross to the oven, stopping briefly beside the bassinet to check on her still-sleeping baby.

Aggie, whose new favorite spot was wherever Noel was, sat beside the bassinet, keeping vigil.

Jillian gave her a quick rub.

Snagging the pot holders from the counter, she removed the baking sheets from the oven, the glorious aroma of cocoa filling the air. Given all the food that had been dropped off since she came home from the hospital, Jillian hadn't needed to do any baking. From the moment she and Noel arrived, not a day had gone by that someone from the church hadn't dropped off food or a gift. Their kindness was surpassed only by the respect they had for her daughter. Aware that she was a preemie, not one person had put Jillian in an awkward position by asking if they could hold Noel.

But chocolate crinkles were Gabriel's favorite, and Jillian wanted to do something special for him. He'd be home soon, and she had a special evening planned. What happened tonight would dictate where she and Gabriel went from here.

Removing the cookies to a cooling rack, Jillian heard Aggie whine. Moments later, a cry echoed from the bassinet.

"Sounds like somebody is hungry."

A knock at the door had Jillian glancing at the clock.

Gabriel was home.

She set the spatula on the counter and hurried to open the door.

Hearing her daughter's pathetic cries, he said, "Uh-oh. Somebody's not happy."

Jillian went to the sink to prepare a bottle. "You mean someone's hungry."

By the time she had the bottle ready, Noel had quieted. Gabriel held her in his arms and spoke softly.

"How do you do that?"

He looked at her. "Do what?"

"Get her to quiet just by talking to her. I mean, if I don't have the bottle ready and waiting, she's not interested in anything I have to say."

He sent a smirk in her direction. "I guess you don't have the touch."

Jillian rolled her eyes and passed him the bottle. "Whatever."

Eyeing the cookies on the counter, he said, "Who are those for?"

"They're a gift."

"For?"

His hopeful gaze suggested he was not going to let this rest. Thankfully, a knock on the door saved her.

She whisked past the table and peered outside to find Rita standing in the porchlight, holding a foil casserole pan.

Jillian opened the door.

"Merry Christmas!" The woman beamed.

"Rita, what are you doing here? I'm the one who should be bringing you food, filling in for me at the library while I'm on maternity leave."

"Oh, honey, we've all been there. It's my pleasure. I'm just thankful you and the baby are healthy."

Jillian held the door as Rita stepped inside.

"Hey, Rita."

"Well, hello, Gabriel. And Merry Christmas. I hear you've been taking very good care of our library director and her little one."

Gabriel wasn't one to blush easily. But he did now. Even the tips of his ears were red.

Hoping to save him, Jillian said, "It pays to have a kindly veterinarian living next door."

"Mmm-hmm." Rita nodded. "I'm sure it does."

Gabriel grew even redder.

"This is my famous Tater Tot casserole." Rita set the pan on the table. "It's still warm, but if you'd prefer to save it, just let it cool, then put it in the freezer."

"No need for that," said Jillian. "We'll have it tonight."

Rita beamed as Gabriel inched a little closer with Noel.

"Say *Thank you, Ms. Rita.*"

"Oh, Gabriel." Rita waved him off. "You are such a mess." Then she winked at Jillian. "He's a natural. You're blessed to have him around."

Jillian couldn't agree more. Which made her even more nervous about telling him how she felt. Because if he didn't feel anything more than friendship, the awkwardness might ruin what they already had.

Once Rita was on her way, Jillian said, "Let me get some plates so we can eat."

"I talked to Mamaw today," he said as she opened the cupboard. "Seems she and Ms. Ida Mae have really taken a liking to online shopping."

Jillian crossed to the table and set the plates down before putting the folded laundry into the basket. "I'm not sure if that's a good thing or a bad thing." Gabriel had brought the grandmas over to meet Noel last night. Not only did they gush nonstop, they were so taken with Noel that they'd asked Gabriel to show them how to shop on their phones so they could buy her some dresses.

"Aw, they're harmless," he said.

"Yes, but there's no telling what sort of damage they'll do to their bank accounts." She pulled the foil off the casserole, then moved beside Gabriel. "Why don't you go ahead and eat? I can take her."

He stared at her. "Jillian, sit down. You don't need to be running around like a chicken with her head cut off."

"Don't you think that's a bit of an exaggeration?"

"Perhaps. But I don't like to see you trying to do everything yourself. You had a baby less than two weeks ago. Cut yourself a little slack, and let me take care of you."

While the thought of him taking care of her had butterflies taking flight in her tummy, she looked up at him. "You do realize I spend at least half of my day on the couch with Noel, right?"

The corners of his mouth twitched. "Good." With Noel on his shoulder, he pulled out a chair and sat down. When she added a serving spoon to the casserole, he immediately scooped a heaping helping onto his plate.

"Do you want me to take her?"

"I'm good."

Yes, he was. No matter which way she looked at him, Gabriel Vaughn was good with a capital *G*. Which was why she'd fallen in love with him.

Over supper, they discussed his plans for the clinic. He'd finally put his mental wish list to paper and was narrowing things down and prioritizing.

Noel was asleep by the time they'd finished eating, so he laid her in the bassinet before putting a few cookies on a plate and bringing them to the table when he again sat down.

With a fortifying breath, she said, "Have I told you how glad I am you're not leaving? You've been so good to me. Done so much for me." She shook her head. "I can't imagine you not being here."

He reached for her hand. "I happen to enjoy helping you."

Suddenly they heard singing.

After exchanging curious looks, he said, "Do you have a speaker on somewhere?"

She shook her head. Yet as her gaze drifted to the window and out into the darkness, she was able to make out a group of people coming up the drive, holding battery-powered candles.

"We have carolers!" Pushing away from the

table, Jillian hurried to open the door. "Come see, Gabriel."

They stepped out onto the side porch as the youth group, led by Ricky and his wife, stopped in front of them and continued singing "Silent Night."

"Sleep in heavenly peace. Sle-ep in heavenly peace."

Gabriel leaned her way. "You won't be sleeping like that for a while."

Laughing, she elbowed him before giving the kids a round of applause. "One more, please. And then I might have some cookies for y'all."

The group clustered to discuss. Moments later, they broke into song. "Up on the housetop reindeer pause."

Gabriel wrapped his arm around her, and she leaned into his warmth wondering if she'd ever experienced such a wonderful Christmas before.

When the kids had finished singing, she went inside and quickly transferred the chocolate crinkles to a platter. Then she brought them outside. "Take as many as you'd like. It'll save me from eating them." She winked at Ricky's wife.

"We have something for you, too." Gloriana's daughter, Kyleigh, stepped forward, holding a gift bag loaded with red and green tissue paper.

Jillian leaned over the railing to accept it. Then

she looked up at Gabriel and said, "What do you think it is?"

"Let's find out." With that, he started flinging tissue paper everywhere.

The kids laughed.

With the tissue gone, Jillian gazed inside. "Ooh." Reaching into the bag, she pulled out a tiny red-and-white sleeper that read My First Christmas. "Aww. It's even got a little stocking cap." Clutching the outfit to her chest, she said, "Thank you all so much. Noel can wear this on Sunday. I'll be sure to take pictures for everyone."

Hands stuffed in the pockets of his jacket, Ricky said, "The kids wanted to say thank you for everything you and Gabriel did to help them with the bazaar."

Beside her, Gabriel frowned. "How come I didn't get a sleeper, then?"

"Trust me." Ricky scoffed. "Nobody wants to see that."

Again, the kids laughed.

After they'd finished their cookies, they went on their way singing "Holly Jolly Christmas," and Jillian and Gabriel went back inside to check on a still-sleeping Noel.

"Aggie makes a pretty good babysitter." He eyed the dog keeping vigil beside the bassinet.

Jillian rubbed her fur. “Without her, I’m not sure where I’d be.”

Gabriel stepped in front of her. “Jillian, there’s something I’d like to discuss with you.”

She sucked in a breath. “If you don’t mind, I have something I need to say first.”

His brow puckered. “Okay.”

Peering into his handsome face, she said, “I love you, Gabriel.”

His green eyes widened. “You—you love me?”

Her insides knotted. This could go either way. “With all of my heart.”

“I don’t understand. When we were discussing Kerrville, you insisted you didn’t need me.”

“Because I refused to stand between you and your dream.”

“Oh, Jillian, don’t you see? I’d rather be doing something less than desirable and be with you than doing anything else without you in my life. *You* are my dream. And knowing that you love me makes me incredibly happy, because I love you, too.” Winding his arms around her waist, he pulled her close. “And have for a very long time. My only regret is not telling you sooner.”

She lifted a brow. “How long?”

“Let’s just say that prior to what I thought was our falling-out back in May, I was exploring the possibility of relocating to Dallas.”

“Why would you do that?”

"Because you wanted to be in Dallas. And I wanted to be with you."

She felt her cheeks heat. "Do you still want to be with me?"

"No. I want to be with both of my girls."

Then he kissed her. Tenderly, yet emphatically, making her glad she'd finally opened up instead of leaving things to wonder. When they parted, he rested his forehead against hers.

Still breathless, she said, "What was it you wanted to talk about?"

He straightened, brushing her hair away from her face. "I thought owning the clinic was my greatest dream. But over the last year, another dream began to take root. And while I tried to fight it, it wouldn't go away."

"What kind of dream?"

"Of sharing my life with a beautiful library director." He reached into his pocket and held up a gold ring with a solitary diamond. "This was Mamaw's engagement ring. She gave it to me today. Said it might come in handy." His smile widened. "I know this might be too soon, but will you marry me, Jillian? Will you be my wife and allow me to be a father to Noel?"

More joy than she'd ever imagined exploded inside of her, bringing tears to her eyes. After all she'd been through, Jillian had wondered if her life would ever be the same. Thankfully, it was not. It was better. God had granted her beauty for ashes. And things she'd once taken for granted she now treasured more than ever. Especially Gabriel.

"Oh, yes." Touching her lips to his, she savored the pleasure of being in his arms. And when she finally forced herself to pull away, she smiled up at him, knowing this Christmas had brought her two of the greatest gifts she could ever receive.

Epilogue

Standing in her kitchen with Aggie beside her, Jillian lit the candle on Noel's birthday cake, finding it hard to believe her little girl was a year old already. And what a year it had been.

The legalities of the clinic were finalized in mid-February, and Gabriel had been like a kid with a new toy when he finally claimed ownership. He'd filled the weeks leading up to that long-hoped-for day by solidifying all of the ideas he'd had tumbling through his mind for the clinic and then winnowing the musts from the wishes before coming up with a plan to execute them. The remodeling and updating began only weeks before their wedding in early April.

Almost as soon as the wedding—which had taken place at the church where she again stood before the congregation with Aggie at her side, only this time as a bride vowing to love her groom until death parted them—was over, Jillian and Gabriel finalized the purchase of Grandmama's house, and then she and Noel packed up and moved into Milly's place with Gabriel while the kitchen, laundry room and bathroom were gutted and remodeled at their new home. Once it was complete, Milly's would serve as a guesthouse whenever their families came to visit.

Before they'd unpacked, though, adoption paperwork had been filed, and in June, Gabriel was legally pronounced Noel's father. Even though she'd always been the daughter of his heart. He'd bonded with her daughter just as much as Jillian had in those final weeks prior to her going back to work at the library.

Once she did, she and Alli Walker agreed to move the Children's Story Hour to twice a month. Except for the six weeks Alli had taken off after the birth of her and Jake's son in June. Jillian had also decided to take a cue from Gloriana and began promoting the library, which had translated into an increase in traffic.

In August, Jillian and Gabriel hosted an openhouse celebration at the newly remodeled Hope Crossing Veterinary Clinic. Though the clinic had remained open throughout the renovations, the event gave the community an opportunity to see the updates that had taken place over the last several months. Aside from their wedding day,

Jillian wasn't sure she'd ever seen her husband so happy. Gabriel was finally living out his dream, and she couldn't be prouder of or happier for him.

By Thanksgiving, they were helping the youth gear up for another Christmas Bazaar. While it had been on a much smaller scale than last year's event, the kids still had fun and came away with funds for next year's mission trip.

Now, as Gabriel and Jillian gathered in their newly renovated kitchen with each of their families, including the grandmas, to celebrate Noel's first birthday, Jillian couldn't help feeling that next year was going to be just as busy.

"What is it, Noel?" While Aggie looked on, making certain her girl was in good hands, Gabriel held his daughter in his lap as she attempted to remove the wrapping paper from one of her many gifts. And by the time he finally helped her pull it off, Noel was far more interested in the colorful paper than the clothing inside.

Jillian held up the adorably frilly dress. "This is so cute. I can't wait for her to wear it."

"I knew the blue would bring out her eyes, the way it always has yours," her mother said.

"Thank you, Mom." Jillian was pleased that, despite their hesitance when they'd first learned she was pregnant, her entire family had embraced Noel. Not only physically but with their whole hearts.

"I don't know about everyone else, but I'm ready for some cake," Grandmama announced after Noel had opened all of her gifts and blown out her candle—with a little help from her father.

"I'm right there with you, Ms. Ida Mae," said Gabriel.

"Gabriel, would you please drop the *Ms.* thing? We're kin now. Call me either Grandmama or Ida Mae."

After passing Noel to Jillian, he stood and moved to her grandmother and gave her a big hug. "You got it, Grandmama." Then he kissed her cheek, and the blush it induced had everyone chuckling.

Jillian handed her daughter to Gabriel's mother before grabbing the plate and starting toward the counter to slice the cake adorned with pink rosettes. "Gabriel, come help me, please."

To her surprise, Aggie followed her instead of remaining with Noel. Then again, the poodle had been clinging to her more lately. And now Jillian knew why.

While the others continued to chat, Gabriel came alongside her, slipping an arm around her waist. "What would you like me to do?"

"Would you get the disposable party plates out of the pantry, please?"

"Sure thing."

Removing the candle from the cake, she watched and waited, until he started her way again.

"What's this?" He held up the small, wrapped box she'd purposely set atop the plates.

"Let me see." Though she already knew. After turning it over, she pointed out the tag she had written his name on and affixed to the bottom. Passing it back to him, she said, "It has your name on it, so I guess you should open it."

He lifted a brow. "Wait a minute, is this one of those ornaments for Daddy's First Christmas or something?"

She shrugged and began slicing the cake. "There's only one way to find out." Then she struggled to keep from giggling while he unwrapped it.

Setting the paper aside, he lifted the lid on the narrow oblong box. Fingering the tissue paper aside, he glanced her way. Then shifted his gaze back to the box and continued to stare. Jillian knew just when he realized what it was.

He jerked his head up, his green eyes wide. "You're pregnant?"

No longer able to contain her smile, she nodded.

"How long have you known?"

"Since early this morning." Though she'd suspected for a couple of weeks.

Setting the box aside, he took her into his arms and kissed her.

Until one of their fathers cleared his throat rather loudly.

"All right, you two," said her dad, "knock it off. We want some cake."

Releasing her, Gabriel licked his lips. "Yes, a celebration like this definitely calls for cake."

Everyone but Noel looked their way.

Then Gabriel returned to the table and took their daughter into his arms. "Guess what, Noel?" His gaze darted to Jillian, his smile wide. "You're going to be a big sister."

For half a second, the room was silent.

Until Gabriel's grandmother said, "Did we call it or what, Ida Mae?"

Everyone looked at the two matriarchs as they high-fived.

"You mean you knew?" Jillian's mother stared at the feisty duo.

Grandmama shrugged. "Suspected."

"But I wasn't even sure until this morning," said Jillian.

"But you've been glowing for days," said Milly.

And as Gabriel moved toward Jillian with Noel still in his arms, Jillian felt as though she truly was glowing. Her heart and her life had never been fuller. What had been intended for evil,

God had used for good. Jillian was a blessed woman, indeed.

Kneeling, she rubbed the soft fur atop Aggie's head. "My friend, it looks as though we're going to be busy." And Jillian wouldn't want it any other way.

* * * * *

If you enjoyed this K-9 Companions book,
be sure to look for
Finding Their Way Back
by Jenna Mindel,
available in January 2024,
wherever Love Inspired books are sold!

And pick up these previous titles in
Mindy Obenhaus's Hope Crossing miniseries:

The Cowgirl's Redemption
A Christmas Bargain
Loving the Rancher's Children

Dear Reader,

I hope you enjoyed this latest visit to Hope Crossing and getting to know a little more about the town's favorite veterinarian. Gabriel is one of those inherently good guys. He's the first to step up when something needs to be done and encourages others to join him. But he wanted somebody to love and be loved in return.

You know, it wasn't until after I'd completed the book that I realized if Gabriel had left the clinic and moved to Dallas to pursue Jillian as he'd been contemplating, he would have traded one dream for another. But circumstances prevented that from happening. And in the end, Gabriel got both of his heart's desires. I love it when God works through *this* lowly vessel (me), to achieve the outcome He desires.

And then there's Jillian. Who wouldn't be terrified after what she endured? But God. As I wrote this book, I kept going back to Joseph's story, his life. So it's no wonder he was often mentioned. God is always at work on behalf of those who love Him. That doesn't mean we won't face trials, but they're a small part of the bigger picture that only God sees. That's why we're called to trust and hold fast to His promises. He will never leave us nor forsake us. He might even send help in the form of a lovable poodle or a couple of understanding (not to mention, scheming) grandmas.

My prayer this Christmas, and throughout the year, is that God will use these words He's given me to bring you joy and remind you of the hope that comes only from knowing His son, Jesus, who stepped down from heaven into the squalor of a stable, walked this earth for thirty-three years, experiencing the same joys and sorrows we face, then died on a cross for our sins, rose again and ascended back into heaven.

Wishing you many blessings,
Mindy